Manolito Four-Eyes

Manolito
Four-Eyes

BY ELVIRA LINDO
ILLUSTRATED BY EMILIO URBERUAGA

TRANSLATED BY JOANNE MORIARTY

MARSHALL CAVENDISH

Marshall Cavendish Corporation
99 White Plains Road
Tarrytown, NY 10591
www.marshallcavendish.us/kids

Library of Congress Cataloging-in-Publication Data
Lindo, Elvira, 1962-
[Manolito Gafotas. English]
Manolito Four-Eyes / by Elvira Lindo ; illustrated by Emilio Urberuaga ; translated by Joanne Moriarty. —1st ed. p. cm.
Summary: Recounts the exploits of the irrepressible Manolito as he navigates the world of his small Madrid neighborhood, along with his grandpa, his little brother, and his school friends.
ISBN 978-0-7614-5303-1
[1. Family life—Spain—Fiction. 2. Grandfathers—Fiction. 3. Schools—Fiction. 4. Spain—Fiction.] I. Urberuaga, Emilio, ill.. II. Moriarty, Joanne. III. Title.
PZ7.L65911Man 2008
[Fic]—dc22
2007028354

The text of this book is set in Adobe Garamond.
Book design by Jay Colvin
Editor: Robin Benjamin

Printed in China
First Marshall Cavendish edition, 2008
Originally published in Spain by Grupo Santillana de Ediciones, S.A., 1994
First edition
10 9 8 7 6 5 4 3 2 1

 **Marshall Cavendish**

For Antonio Muñoz Molina,
my life

CAST OF CHARACTERS

Manolito Four-Eyes
A ten-year-old boy from
Carabanchel, he's a chatterbox
who's misunderstood.

Grandpa Nicolás
Manolito's unconditional ally

The Bozo
Manolito's favorite little
brother—he only has one!

The One-and-Only Susana

This girl is like a whirlwind.
Her limitless imagination
can get anyone in trouble,
especially Manolito.

Ozzy

The biggest bully and
troublemaker in
Manolito's school

Big Ears

A despicable traitor and
Manolito's inseparable
friend

Miss Asunción

Even though she thinks
all her students are
delinquents, she never
loses hope that
they'll change.

Manolito Four-Eyes

1

The Number-One Bum

My name is Manolito García Moreno, but if you come to my neighborhood and ask the first guy that passes by, "Excuse me, please, Manolito García Moreno?"—one of two things will happen. The guy will shrug, or he'll mutter something like: "Hey, beats me."

That's because nobody knows me as Manolito García Moreno, not even Big Ears López, and he's my best friend; even though sometimes he can be a dog and a traitor (and other times, a dog traitor), he's still my best friend and he's a whole lotta cool.

In Carabanchel—that's the name of my neighborhood in Madrid, in case I haven't told you—everyone knows me as Manolito Four-Eyes. Everyone who *knows* me, of course. People who don't know me don't know that I've worn glasses since I was five years old. Well, that's their loss.

I was named Manolito after my dad's truck, and the truck was named after my dad, whose name is Manolo. My dad was named after his dad, and so on back to the beginning of time. In other words, in case Steven Spielberg wants to know, the first velociraptor was called Manolo, and that's the way it went right on up until today. Until Manolito García number one—that's me, the Number-One Bum. That's what my mother calls me in certain crucial moments, and she doesn't call me that because she's a sociologist researching the origins of humanity. She calls me it when she's about to start one of her world-famous lectures. It bugs me that she calls me Number-One Bum, and it bugs her that people call me Four-Eyes. Obviously, different things bug us, even though we're from the same family.

Manolito Four-Eyes

I like that they call me Four-Eyes. At my school—which is called Diego Velázquez—anyone who's a little important has a nickname. Before I had a nickname, I used to cry plenty. When a bully started in on me at recess, he always ended up calling me Four-Eyes or Fat Glasses. Since I've officially become Manolito Four-Eyes, insulting me is a waste of time. They could call me Fathead, too, but it hasn't occurred to them yet, and you can bet I'm not about to give them any clues. The same thing happened to my pal Big Ears López; ever since he got his nickname, nobody really gets on his case about his ears.

One day Big Ears and I got into a kicking fight on the way home from school because he said he'd rather have his ears over my Coke-bottle glasses, and I said I'd rather have

my Coke-bottle glasses over his monkey-butt ears. He didn't like that "monkey butt" thing at all, but it's true—it's been certified by a notary. When it's cold out, his ears turn the same color as the monkeys' butts at the zoo. Big Ears' mom told him not to worry, because when you get older, your ears shrink, and if they don't shrink, a surgeon trims them, and all's well that ends well.

Big Ears' mom is a whole lotta cool because she's divorced and since she feels guilty, she never chews out Big Ears. She doesn't want him to have an even bigger trauma than the one currently being cured by Miss Esperanza, our school psychologist. My mom doesn't want me to have traumas either, but since she's not divorced, every now and again she chews me out, which is her specialty.

It's not just because she's my mom; the truth is, she's an expert like no other. My grandpa doesn't like how my mom chews me out, and he always tells her, "If you're gonna do it, do it later, woman." My grandpa calls her the Colonel, but only behind her back. He doesn't dare say it to her face, even though he's her dad. She's the Colonel for a reason.

My grandpa's cool; he's so cool, he's a whole lotta cool. Three years ago he moved back from his village, and my mom closed off the terrace with exposed aluminum and put in a sofa bed so that my grandpa and I could sleep out there. Every night I fold out the bed. It's a deadly pain, but I just grin and bear it because afterward my grandpa always gives me a ten-cent coin for my pig—it's not a real pig; it's a piggy bank—and I'm getting filthy rich.

Sometimes he calls me the crown prince, since he says that everything he has saved up from his pension will go to me. My mom doesn't like us to talk about death, but my grandpa says in the last year of his life, he plans on talking about whatever he wants.

My grandpa always says he wants to die before the year 2010; he doesn't feel like seeing what will happen in the next decade; and when it comes to decades, he's already had enough with this one. He's determined to die in 2009 from his bad prostate. He says he's spent so much time dealing with the pain-in-the-neck prostate, it would be a real drag to die from something else.

I've told him that I'd rather inherit all his pension without him dying, because sleeping on the terrace with my Grandpa Nicolás is so cool, it's a whole lotta cool. Every night we go to sleep with the radio on, and if my mom tries to turn it off, we wake up. That's just how we are. If my grandpa died, I'd have to share the terrace with the Bozo, and *that* would ruin all the fun.

The Bozo is my little baby brother, the only one I have. My mom doesn't like how I call him the Bozo (there's really no nickname that she gets a kick out of). Just to set the record straight, I started to call him that without realizing it. It wasn't one of those times when you do heavy thinking with your fists holding your head up so it won't explode. The nickname just popped out the day he was born:

My grandpa took me to the hospital. I was five years old. I remember because I had just broken in my first pair of glasses, and Our Nosy Neighbor Luisa was always saying,

"It's okay that his dad wears glasses, but that poor little thing, he's only five." Anyway, I went up to the crib and I put in my hand. I was going to open his eye, because Big Ears had told me that if my little brother had red eyes, that meant he was possessed by the devil. I went to do it, with the best of intentions, and the dude started to cry with that fake bawling of his. Then everyone jumped on me as if I were the one possessed, and for the first time I thought, "What a Bozo!" And it's just one of those things that get stuck in your head.

So nobody can say I gave him the nickname on purpose. It was all him. He was born to bug me, and he deserves it.

Just like I deserve my grandpa calling me Manolito the New Joselito. It's from my grandpa's favorite song, which he taught me, called "The Bell Ringer." It's a really ancient song, from back when there was no bathroom in my grandpa's house and the TV was "silent." Some nights we play like I am Joselito, who was the ancient boy who sang the song in the past, and I sing it and then I make like I'm flying and things like that—because if I don't play like I'm Joselito, once we finish singing "The Bell Ringer," it turns into a bore galore. Not only that—my grandpa's eyes well up because of how old "The Bell Ringer" is and because the ancient kid ends up in jail, and I get embarrassed that my grandpa cries, what with how old he is, over such an ancient kid.

Summing it up, if you go to Carabanchel and you ask for Manolito the New Joselito, they're not gonna tell you anything or they might point you to the jail in my neighborhood, just to be funny, which is a habit people have.

They won't know who Manolito García Moreno is, or the New Joselito, but everyone will give you the ins and also the outs of Manolito, otherwise known on this side of the River Manzanares as Four-Eyes, and even better-known in his own house as "Look who's talking, the Number-One Bum."

2

Manolito's Anchor

At the beginning of September, my mom sent my grandpa and me to buy a button with an anchor on it that was missing from my peacoat. Big Ears López ripped it off last year—he bit it after I refused to give him my crispy, crunchy baguette. He broke a tooth and I lost my anchor. His mom consoled him and mine chewed me out (one of those delayed-reaction lectures that I don't realize has started until half an hour in). That day I learned that if you want to have your mother in the palm of your hand, it's much better to break something in your body than to break something off your clothes. They have issues with clothes. On the other hand, as soon as their kids get careless, they start bragging about their injuries:

"Yesterday, my son broke his tooth."

"Big deal—mine broke his leg."

Mothers never like to come in last when they're with other mothers. That's why when September came, my mom said to me, "I don't want you to start school and end up in October before I sew the anchor on your peacoat."

It was my peacoat from last year; it'll be the one this year; and it'll be the one next year and the next and the next, because my mom says that kids grow fast and you have to buy peacoats with the future in mind. Kids grow fast, but not me. That's why this will be the peacoat I wear until the day I die when I'm old. I hate my peacoat. I'll have to spend my whole life hating the same peacoat. How boring!

This summer, my mom made the doctor prescribe me vitamins. I think she's embarrassed that the peacoat is still big on me, and she gives me vitamins so the peacoat and I will be the same size once and for all. There are times when I think my mom loves the peacoat more than she loves me, and I'm her flesh and blood. I asked my grandpa about this while we were going to get the button, but he told me that all mothers get attached to peacoats, coats in general, and hats and gloves, but that through it all, they still love their children most because mothers have big hearts.

In my neighborhood, Carabanchel, there's a little of everything. There's a jail, buses, kids, inmates, mothers, criminals, and bread stores, but there aren't any anchor buttons for peacoats, so my Grandpa Nicolás and I caught the subway to go downtown. We're pretty lucky with the subway—even when it's really full, people feel sorry for both of us, and they always let us sit down. They feel sorry for my grandpa because he's old and has a bad prostate. You can't see his prostate, but you can see that he's old. Maybe they feel sorry for me because I wear glasses; I can't really guarantee that.

When people let us sit down, we feel obligated to put on poor-chump faces. Otherwise, for instance, if they let

you sit down and right away you start cracking up, people get peeved. That's why my grandpa and I always get on the train like we're a wreck, and it always pays off. Try it, but don't go around telling everyone, or else the word will get out and the deal's off.

My mom sent us to Pontejos, a store in the Puerta del Sol square in Madrid, where all the mothers in the world-wide world go to buy buttons, zippers, needles, and anchors. We spent an hour in front of the counter because my grandpa let all the ladies cut the line. He loves when ladies cut, and if they have time, when they stay and have a coffee with him. No lady has ever had the time for coffee with my grandpa, but he says he'll never give up.

After an hour of my grandpa talking with one lady after another, I lay down on the counter. I was really tired from standing up. The salesman tried his best to get rid of us. I think he didn't want me to put my boots on the counter. When we finally had the anchor button in our possession, my grandpa said, "We've fulfilled our responsibilities. Now let's take a stroll around Grand Street, Manolito."

And I answered him, "Okay. How cool, dearest grand-father."

Well, I didn't say "dearest grandfather." If I ever actually said "dearest grandfather" to my grandpa, he'd rush me with utmost urgency to the hospital.

We went to Grand Street, which is one of the busiest and nicest shopping areas. And what do you think we saw? A protest. We have protests in my neighborhood, but they're not as nice as the ones they have on Grand Street.

My grandpa said, "Let's stick around and take up space."

It must've seemed fine to the people protesting—they

didn't kick us out or anything. My grandpa asked a man to put me up on his shoulders so that I could see what was happening. I never did figure out what they were protesting, but when I was up there, I noticed that the guy had dandruff. I asked him why he didn't buy one of those shampoos they advertise on TV that gets rid of dandruff (and if you don't watch out, gets you a girlfriend, too).

The guy put me down on the ground, all in a huff, and said, "The grandkid's real heavy."

That creep was going to give me a fat complex again! You see, every once in a while, I get a complex. I've had them about being short, fat, four-eyed, clumsy . . . I won't go on, because I'm bad-mouthing myself. The fat complex came on really strong last year, but I got over it because the truth is, it's ridiculous to have a fat complex.

My grandpa didn't hear what the dandruff guy said because he was busy complaining about his pension, which is what he always does when he finds himself with more than two people. Then he talks about how since the pressure cooker was imposed upon us, society has lost a lot.

During the protest, we walked in the middle of the street, with no cars. The street was full of police, and I thought, "How cool!" After a while, the protest finished, and my grandpa said, "I'm gonna buy you a hamburger so your mother doesn't say I starve you to death."

He bought me a hamburger, and he ordered three ice creams, two for him—since he's got a bad prostate—and one for me, since I'm a bit fat. And I thought, "How cool, how cool is the world, the ball of the world, how cool!" It was the most important day of my life.

All of a sudden, I got the giggles and started jumping around.

My grandpa said, "Don't jump. You can't jump on Grand Street. The subway's below us, and this thing can go under from less than nothing."

So I held back a smidgen, and I only jumped mentally. I'm pretty used to jumping mentally. If I don't, Our Nosy Neighbor Luisa comes up to ask "What on God's green Earth is that—an earthquake from San Francisco?"

I swear that we were heading home, but then we saw a lady that does the newscasts sitting in a café eating a BLT. I know that's what she was eating, because my grandpa and I stood there watching through the window until she finished.

You could tell she was embarrassed; the lady didn't know which way to look. In the middle of it all, a little mayo fell onto her chin, and she wiped it off quickly. She called the waiter over and signaled for him to close the curtains, but she was out of luck, because there were no curtains.

I couldn't leave until she got up. In my school, kids say that a lot of newscasters don't have legs—and that's why they become newscasters, because they don't *need* their legs. My friends never would've forgiven me if I had left without proving this. And in order to prove things like that, you have to go to downtown Madrid, where the stars are. In my neighborhood, Carabanchel, there are no anchor buttons and no stars.

The waiter came out and said to my grandpa, "Grandpops, if you wanna see animals, take the kid to the zoo. This is a café."

And without skipping a beat, my grandpa said, "I'm with my grandson in the street, and nobody can kick me out of the street—not you nor the mayor, even if he showed up here *en persona*."

My grandpa threw out *en persona* without batting an eye. He never puts on airs.

But the waiter stayed in command-mode. He was the typical brown-noser around stars. He went on, "I'm responsible for this young lady having a sandwich in peace, not like a monkey in a cage."

"That monkey comment came out of your mouth, not mine," said my grandpa, who speaks better than the president. "But I don't know why the young lady is so embarrassed by a poor old man and a boy watching her eat when every night, millions of viewers devote their undivided attention to her mouth."

"Well, it just bothers her," said the waiter, who was about to win the prize for pain-in-the-neck of the year *and* typical star brown-noser.

"It bothers me more," my grandpa said to the waiter— and to everyone else that had gathered around us by

now—"it bothers me more," he repeated, "that the young lady makes a mistake every five seconds in the news, because I am a taxpayer who pays his taxes even though his pension doesn't cover the cost of an Ace bandage. Let the young lady talk about pensions in her newscast."

When my grandpa finished saying that, the crowd applauded more than at the rally a little while before. My poor grandpa's chin quivers when he gets excited, and it was quivering then.

The crowd told the waiter to get him a glass of water, and so the waiter was out of luck and had to go into the café for a glass of water—but he wasn't the one who came out holding the glass.

You're not gonna believe it, but I swear to the Bozo that the one who brought the glass was the newscaster lady. It was a crucial moment in our lives.

"Take this," she said to my grandpa in the same tone of voice she has on TV. "Are you feeling better?"

My grandpa said yes; that he only wanted to show his grandson that newscasters have legs, and on top of that, very pretty ones; that there aren't any other reporters like her, and the TV doesn't do her justice; that she was a hundred times more beautiful in person and good night; that the boy is starting school, we've come downtown to get an anchor button and look at the time, my daughter will be calling the police.

After wrapping up his second speech, he drank two more sips of water and we began walking. My grandpa raised his hand in the middle of Grand Street to catch a taxi. Without a doubt, we were already mega-late.

A taxi stopped, and he said to the driver, "Listen, we're going to Upper Carabanchel. Do you think two Euros will cover the ride?"

And the taxi driver answered, "No, that's out in the boondocks."

The taxi driver refused to take us and didn't even say good-bye. There are people who get mad just because you ask them a simple question. There are people in the world who act really stinky.

"What with the hamburger, we have only two measly Euros left, Manolito," my grandpa said. The dude blamed my hamburger. He didn't remember that he'd wolfed down two ice creams.

So we had to go back the way we came, on the subway. I got really sleepy. I got really sleepy thinking about school, about my teacher, about the winter, and about my peacoat. And if you're thinking about all that and you're on the subway to boot, your head gets mushy and you can't think at all.

The same thing must've been happening to my grandpa, because he said, "I'm gonna catch forty winks, Manolito, sweetie. Watch out so we don't pass our stop."

But I fell asleep, too, deep asleep . . . and then, even deeper asleep.

A subway guard woke us both up. We'd ended up in the

middle of a field, and we didn't know what time it was. There's nothing worse than falling asleep on the subway and waking up in the middle of a field. I started to cry before anyone could chew me out. But the guard didn't chew us out—he told us we had reached the field house, where the subway cars are kept, and then he came with us to the nearest station (apparently he could tell my grandpa had a bad prostate) where we could catch a ride back.

When we got home, all our neighbors were on the stoop consoling my mom about our disappearance. Our Nosy Neighbor Luisa had told my mom, "Don't worry, Cata. If they were dead, they would've already been on the news."

Everyone chewed out my grandpa: that he was clueless, that the boy had to get up early, that we must not've had dinner, that they were about to call the special police rescue team. My grandpa went running up the stairs ("running" is a manner of speaking) to get away from the crowd.

When we'd been in the house awhile, and my mom had thrown everything since the day we were born in our faces, it occurred to her to ask, "What about the anchor button for the peacoat?"

The anchor was nowhere in sight. She said that one day we were going to kill her from aggravation and a deadly heart attack.

That night, for the first time since summer began, my grandpa left his socks on to sleep; I know because I sleep on the sofa bed with him. In my neighborhood, Carabanchel, as soon as school starts, the cold starts. That's just the way it is; it's been proven by scientists all around the world.

A while went by, two whiles; after the third while, I realized that I couldn't sleep. You see, school started the next day, and everyone would have so many things to tell each other, they might not care about every exciting thing that had happened to me on Grand Street. I thought all that to myself because I thought my grandpa had already fallen asleep.

But suddenly, he said in my ear, "What a great time we had today, Manolito, sweetie. Tomorrow when I tell them in the senior center that the newscaster lady brought me a glass of water, they're not gonna believe it. Thank God I have a witness."

Then he didn't say anything else. He fell asleep. I could tell because he was making the weird noise he makes when he takes out his teeth to sleep. The radio announcer said something about kids having school the next day. What a great guy; he had to remind me of the most miserable part of my future.

Well, going back to school had its good points, too: I'd see Big Ears . . . Big Ears, who I'd seen all summer, what a pain in the neck. . . . But there was also the One-and-Only Susana. . . .

I also realized that my grandpa had gone to bed without taking off his hat. He did that whenever something important happened to him. At least he had his head covered up. My grandpa had lost whatever it is in your head that holds teeth on the inside and hair on the outside. As you saw, he lost whatever it is that holds your tongue, too.

I was falling asleep, at last, when I realized that I had something in my hand. . . . It was the anchor! It turned out I hadn't let go of it all afternoon. My mom could sew it on my peacoat the next day. She could relax.

I had experienced the most important day of my life, but it didn't matter. Nobody could save me from school, or my teacher, or the winter, or my peacoat.

That was the worst—nobody could save me from my peacoat.

3

What an Idiotic Diagnosis

The One-and-Only Susana says that when people from Spain go to the psychologist, it's because they've already been kicked out of everywhere else; that before they used to send you to a really deserted island, but now, with the number of people in the world, there aren't any more deserted islands; and that's why psychologists have to exist.

We put up with these theories because she's a girl. If she were a boy, we'd make him bite the dust, jerk.

She said this to Big Ears López (my best friend, even though he's a dog traitor), to Ozzy (the bully of my neighborhood), and to me (as I've already told you a thousand times, I'm Manolito Four-Eyes). And she told it to us two weeks ago while we were waiting for the school psychologist to see us—to see us one at a time because no one can stand to see the three of us together. Between now and three years, at the latest, we'll end up delinquents. That's not what I say, Miss Asunción says so. In addition to being Our Teach, she's also a futurologist: she sees the future of all her students. She doesn't need a crystal ball or tarot cards; she digs her eyes into your head, and she sees you years from now as one of the most-wanted delinquents in history or winning one Nobel Prize after another. She doesn't have a middle ground.

Since his parents are divorced, Big Ears' mother took him to the school psychologist so he wouldn't have a terrible trauma and become a serial killer when he's older. As far as Ozzy's concerned, Miss Asunción says he's been an

agitator and a bully since he could walk. One day Our Teach had us draw our parents, and Ozzy drew his mom with a moustache and his dad with horns; Our Teach doesn't like mothers to be in drawings without shaving first. We thought it was really really really funny; if there'd been a European Idol Contest of family drawings, for sure Ozzy would've taken first prize. But Our Teach, who always has to ruin the best Kodak moments, took the drawing away from him, kept it, and called his parents—so that she could see the moustache and horns in real life. You could see the moustache on his mom a little, but when it came to the horns on his father—nothing. What a bummer. (I'm telling all this in case someone cares.)

My mom took me to the psychologist because I never stop talking, and she says I make her head mushy and that, when I'm not talking, I flip my lid right outta Madrid—in other words, I freak out. My mom says all that about me; that's why she took me to the psychologist. She must've thought, "Whatever he talks about with her, he won't have to talk about at home." But she was wrong. I only went to the psychologist twice, and when I got home, I felt like talking even more because, as my grandpa says, "All the boy's ideas get trapped in his noggin."

Even though the psychologist is called Miss Espe, she always says, "Call me Esperanza." But that doesn't go over big in my school. If your name is Esperanza, you'll be Miss Espe until the day you die, and if not, then why were you born anyway? So sorry.

Going to Miss Espe was fantastic. Picture this: I went in and asked with all the politeness I've ever been taught, "What do I have to do, Miss Espe?"

She repeated that she wasn't a "Miss" and she wasn't "Espe," but it didn't do any good. When I get used to something, it's pretty hard for it to be any other way. Like what happened to me with the Bozo. "Don't call your brother Bozo," everyone in Spain tells me; but I don't do it to offend anyone; I do it because by now I don't remember his real name.

Miss Espe told me that she was there in her office so that I could tell her all my problems.

"You want me to tell you them all, since the day I was born?" I asked.

I asked that because I like to make things clear from the beginning of time. And because the truth is: I'm a real riot. But Miss Espe didn't care; she wanted to know everything I had to tell her; and she told me to take all the time I wanted—that she was there to listen to me. I thought, "How cool!"

Before I started telling the story of my life, I asked her, "Can I smoke in here?"

She looked at me as if suddenly I had two heads, and she proceeded to tell me that children don't smoke. What a genius. I had to tell her it was just one of my little jokes so she'd close her mouth—because she left it wide open, poor Miss Espe. I felt so bad for her, falling for such a dumb joke, a joke that my mom and Miss Asunción already knew, a joke no one has ever fallen for and no one gets a kick out of; I felt so bad for her that I started to tell her the story of my life.

I started from when my parents asked for a loan to buy the truck and they named it Manolito, and then they gave that name to me, the boy who couldn't decide whether to come out of dead man's limbo—which is where all children wait around, floating, before they're born. Ozzy the Bully told me that last bit; he told me he still remembers when he was in dead man's limbo. There you are, floating in your own little world, and one day a huge, giant-sized hand goes and says, "You"—it says "you" because at that point nobody has a name—"it's your turn."

And that's when you get astrally transported to an operating room in a hospital, and a doctor smacks you on your rear end. Why? Because you're born. From that crucial moment, your life starts in Carabanchel or in Hollywood, depending on where the giant-sized hand takes you. As for me, the hand brought me to Carabanchel. But I recommend you don't believe it all, because Ozzy the Bully always comes out with stories like that just to shoot the breeze; I'm warning you, and he who warns is not a traitor.

Anyway, back to where I left off—all of a sudden, I was born. I told Miss Espe how they had to perform a life-or-death operation on my mom so I could be born. Apparently, I had what could be called a somewhat fat head. My mom really likes to tell that one to make me look ridiculous.

I told Miss Espe that for the first three months, I was famous for not letting anyone in my building sleep because I cried so much, and how one day, I laughed so hard that I lost consciousness. I told her that my mom said, "This one—he's me—he was born talking."

Well, I told her everything I knew up until I was three or four years old. Then Miss Espe, who looked like she still hadn't come out of dead man's limbo herself, told me I could go.

I asked her, "Why, Miss Espe? Is it that I'm not explaining all the details well?"

"You're explaining everything marvelously," Miss Espe said. "It's just that an hour and a half has gone by."

An hour and a half! It had flown by. I think that hour and a half was the happiest hour and a half of my life. Miss Espe said good-bye, yawning. My mom would say, "That's from hunger, sleepiness, or not enough sleep." It must've been hunger.

I was really happy. I had shone. I'd explained everything to her like in the movies, from before the protagonist is born. I even told her about when my parents closed off the terrace with exposed aluminum so my grandpa and I could sleep out there, which is something my mom's friends talk about a lot—about when they close off terraces and when they tile the floor. Miss Espe told me to come back the next week.

All throughout the week, I wrote down the things I remembered from when I was three to ten years old. I asked my grandpa, my parents, Our Nosy Neighbor Luisa, and everyone that's been lucky enough to know me since I was born. I finished the notebook in two days. My mom bought me another double-lined notebook; she said I needed it for the sessions with Miss Espe.

When I went back to Miss Espe's office, I had three double-lined notebooks about my life and all of its problems. I'd put a title on each notebook. The first one was about when I was three to five years old, and I called it:

My life without the Bozo

That notebook dealt with what the world was like before it occurred to the Bozo to come out of dead man's limbo, and how good people were back then: they always said please, there weren't any kidnappings, motorcycles had mufflers, there was no hunger in Africa, and the bathroom didn't have the leak that drives my mom up the wall. Whenever the Bozo or I cry, my grandpa tells us, "The leak in the bathroom is from the guy upstairs. He always misses the toilet when he pees."

The dude tells us that because he knows that no matter how much we're crying, we have to fall on the floor cracking up immediately. My mom fumes and tells my grandpa, "That's all they need, for you to tell them filthy things; they're already filthy enough as it is."

Before the Bozo existed, I wasn't as filthy. I swear. But one fine day, you discover that your brother laughs the hardest when you say something filthy, so you get all excited hoping to crack him up.

I don't know if I told Miss Espe that last part about the leak in the bathroom, because in the second session I had with her I only had time to read the first notebook. While I was reading, I sometimes got the impression that Miss Espe was nodding off, like my grandpa does after eating. I asked Miss Espe if she was nodding off because she had a bad prostate. She said she wasn't nodding off (just to set the record straight—yes, she was), that she didn't have a bad prostate, that no women have bad prostates, that the hour was over, and that I didn't need to come back.

Miss Espe didn't find any traumas in me. But I don't think she looked hard enough. She told my mom that the only thing I had was a desire to talk, an enormous desire to talk; that I was dying to talk, and that rather than a disease, it's more like a bug you have—like a stomach bug. What an idiotic diagnosis—I could make a diagnosis like that, big deal.

Miss Espe told my mom that the only thing I needed was to be listened to more at home. My mom said, "More???"

At recess, Ozzy the Bully said that Miss Espe had gotten rid of the hassle of putting up with me for an hour and a half every week. He was showing off because he hadn't gotten kicked out—yet. Only me. *Only me.* If I didn't wear glasses, I might've fought him; but I'm tired of paying for it from both ends: from Ozzy and from my mom when she sees my glasses broken. I'm in favor of those that turn the other cheek.

My dad says, "What you have to do is stand up to them if they hit you."

To pay for it again? No way, José.

Anyway, the truth is, that bit with Miss Espe didn't

sit well with me at all. Imagine you go to have a urine analysis, and you get the result and you read:

> You are a royal pain.
> Doctor Martinez

That hurts. It must not have sat well with my mom, either. She said, "That lady's gonna tell me I don't listen to this boy. He won't even let me put in a load of laundry."

In the end I had to start crying. (You would've done the same thing.)

That night, my mom said that everyone was going to listen to me, so that no stranger could go around saying that nobody listened to me at home. Everyone came in my room. I was a little embarrassed. My grandpa was lying down next to me on the bed. My mom was sitting on the bed, holding the Bozo, and my dad lay down next to her.

They said, "Speak."

I don't like to improvise. I grabbed my double-lined notebooks and read to them. When I started on the second notebook, I was interrupted by my dad's snoring. The guy snores like a walrus. I didn't know what to do then since they'd all taken over the bed. So I went to my parents' bed, and I left them there all balled up and sleeping peacefully. I did shut off the light, turn off the radio, and put my grandpa's comforter over them. For sure my mom would wake up saying that all the bones in her "bodily body" were aching. Oh, so sorry—that's what they get for not listening to the story of my life to the very end. I was gonna start thinking that my notebooks would put even sheep to sleep.

The next morning I'd get chewed out by my family. I didn't know why, but for sure I'd get chewed out. You can sense it the same way that you sense you're about to get a zero on a test. The One-and-Only Susana says that when someone's been kicked out of everywhere, that's when they get taken to the psychologist, and before now, they used to get taken to deserted islands. If I had to choose between Miss Espe and a deserted island, I'd go with . . . my parents' bed. It's the biggest deserted island I've seen in my life, and it's only a 54 x 75 inch double bed for affectionate marriages. (According to my mom, that bit about affectionate marriage is only a manner of speaking.)

4

Captain Lush

A few days ago I didn't go to school—my dad and I had an appointment with the optometrist because of this kid who's beyond the law, Captain Lush. These were terrifying days, when violence erupted in my life. I wish Rambo were put in some of the terrible situations I've been in. The guy would hide his tail between his legs.

I'm gonna tell you this story from the beginning of time. Picture this: I was in Hangman's Park (we call it that because it only has one tree, so it looks a bit suspicious). I didn't have a care in the world. I was with Big Ears López, playing with my truck, when Ozzy the Bully came up without prior warning, stomped on the honker—on the truck's honker, not mine—and said: "Now we're gonna make believe I'm Captain America." After giving this order in no uncertain terms, he pointed to Big Ears and added: "This one's the girl, and Manolito's the dirty traitor, and I fight him to the death. I end up with the girl, and Manolito ends up flat on the ground with his bones broken."

Ozzy's like that—he likes the premise of the game to be clear from the start.

Seeing as I was gonna get annihilated, I said, "Well, I'd kinda rather be the girl."

But that dirty coward Big Ears was thrilled with the role Ozzy had dished out to him. "No, I'll be the girl. I'll be the bee's knees. I'll win the Hollywood Oscar for Best Supporting Actress."

I looked at him, my eyes flooded with hatred, and it occurred to me to ask, "Or what about putting the game off till tomorrow? It's just—I have to prepare myself psychologically."

Tough guy Ozzy answered: *"Now."*

So Big Ears began his role of the princess getting attacked, screaming as if he'd been wound up, and I took off running as if I were gonna win the hundred-yard dash. I'm one of those guys that likes to fight while backpedaling. But in life, people are divided in two groups: the ones that win races, and the ones that lose them. And I'm in the second group.

Ozzy the Bully grabbed me by the collar of my peacoat

and said, "Defend yourself, Four-Eyes. You have the opportunity to fight the biggest animal in the class, and that's me."

Well, if you looked at it like that, it was a stroke of luck. Obviously, bragging about Rambo giving you a black eye is better than having to confess that it was Tweety Bird who made you kiss the dirt.

I couldn't defend myself with my hands—my whole body was paralyzed by the intense emotion of that crucial moment of my life—so I had to defend myself with my mouth; it's the only thing that responds when I'm about to die. When I say I defended myself "with my mouth," I don't mean by biting—don't be such an animal. I mean by talking:

"It's just that I'm the king, and nobody can hit the king; it's prohibited by the Constitution; so if you hit me, you'll wind up in jail, and the entire population of Spain will turn against you."

You have to admit, if there were a World Series of statements on this planet, mine would at least make it to the finals. But Ozzy's not impressed by great statements; he's the classic tough guy, a hard nut to crack.

He said, "No way you're gonna be king; kings can't wear glasses, and when a king is born needing glasses, they send that king to a different country and they get another one."

Now that was something I didn't expect. My dad had told me that he'd gotten out of military service because of his glasses, but I didn't know that because of glasses you couldn't become king (an occupation, by the way, that I'd never thought about, but in that moment it seemed to me the only occupation that was worthwhile in the world, if it could get rid of a dangerous guy like Ozzy).

Once I saw a guy on TV who was saying how, one time, he was in a plane, without a care in the world, when all of a sudden the pilot announces on the loudspeakers that the motors are failing and they have to do the classic emergency landing. The guy (who was American, but not an actor) said that while the plane was nose-diving, he thought, "These are the final moments of my life." And then, everything he'd done since the day he was born flashed through his mind like a movie. Well, that's exactly what happened to me, but opposite: Just when that animal Ozzy was holding me by my peacoat, and I was about to fall with my bones broken on the ground, my life flashed in front of me like a movie—but instead of going backward, it went forward. I saw my future; I saw entire days inside my head, but they went by at such a high speed that I almost don't remember anything. I only remember two things: that I became king, and that my family and I were on TV after the nighttime news, just like the king and queen of Spain. I was in the middle, with the typical king's cape and the crown tilted a little to the side (which is how I like to wear crowns); my grandpa was next to me in his Sunday best; and my parents were standing up, my mom holding the Bozo. We were all smiling, and the anthem of Spain played in the background: "Chunda, chunda, tachunda chunda, chunda, tatachundachun. Tachunda chundachun—!"

But then Ozzy the Bully grabbed me tighter around my neck, and my mind had to come back to reality.

So Ozzy said that kings couldn't wear glasses. Luckily, I have reflexes, and I challenged him: "That's a lie, look at King Baudouin."

That's what you call a low blow. I remember Baudouin, the king of Belguim, because Our Nosy Neighbor Luisa says she cried intensely when he died. She spent her summers in Andalucía on the coast of Spain, like his majesty; and she says he was a very good person because he married a Spanish woman, but that the poor thing was one of those Spanish women who aren't very pretty. Luisa says that in Andalucía they lived right next door to each other. My mom always whispers behind her: "Yeah, right next door. C'mon, don't tell me that one doesn't have a good imagination."

Manolito Four-Eyes

Ozzy the Bully was sick of Baudouin and his glasses. He said, "You still wanna be king, Four-Eyes?"

He calls me Four-Eyes all the time, so that was nothing new. But I made a historic mistake and said yes. Don't go thinking he warned me—he punched me smack in the right lens of my glasses and turned around to leave, saying, "Mission accomplished."

Apparently, there are kids whose mission is to punch me in Hangman's Park.

At that painful moment in my life, I saw my grandpa walking up. I thought my back was covered, and I yelled at Ozzy, "You'll never be Captain America! The only thing you'll ever be in your life is Captain Lush! The whole world will know you as Captain Lush!"

You see, everyone in Stumbles Bar calls his dad Lush, and not exactly because he's a conservationist saving the lush tropical rain forests of Brazil.

That must have hurt Ozzy as much as his punch hurt me—because he came back and, in front of my grandpa, took off my glasses and threw them with perfect aim so that they ended up hanging from Hangman's Tree.

Of course, my grandpa couldn't run after him (because of his bad prostate), and I was left like a kid who says he has an uncle in Waikiki; I didn't have an uncle, and I didn't have diddly. The glasses were so high up, my grandpa and I had to get them down by throwing rocks.

We went back home. First my mom hugged me when she saw what happened to my eye, and then she chewed me out when she saw what happened to my glasses.

My grandpa shouted, "Don't you go lecturing him! He's gotten enough misery for today."

In the end, everyone was giving me sympathy and explaining the TV shows to me because without my glasses, I'm as blind as a bat.

All of a sudden, without prior warning, my dad rolled up his sleeves and announced, "Manolito, I'm going to teach you the typical García punch, so that neither the Lush's son nor any other father's son makes you bite the dust again."

Not just because he's my dad, but the classic García punch is amazing! It was the best punch I'd ever seen in my life.

First he gave me a class on theory: "You have to make your enemy believe that you're gonna hit him with the left, and when he goes to defend his left side, you sock him with a tremendous right."

I only needed three more classes of theory because on the fourth one, he said, "Now, Manolito, show me what Manolo García's son is capable of."

It was my first professional punch.

I broke his glasses. I don't know how I managed to break both lenses at the same time. Unsolved mysteries.

Nothing else occurred to me but to ask, "How did I do?"

My dad answered softly, very softly, "Go to bed, Manolito."

I went running into bed. I covered my entire mega-head with the covers, and I thought, "I wish I could wake up at least two months from now, after this evil day."

But my ears still worked, and I heard my mom in the hallway saying to my dad, "You two must've decided to make the optometrist a millionaire!"

My whole body started itching. The same thing always happens when I'm nervous—I have to scratch and scratch, just like an abandoned dog with fleas in the middle of a highway.

"If you keep scratching yourself like that, you're gonna bleed," said grandpa from his side of the bed.

"It's just that I can't fall asleep. It's Ozzy's fault I have to go to sleep without my glasses! It's Ozzy's fault I broke Dad's glasses; and the kicker is, when I go back to school,

I'll have to see Ozzy and I'll be trapped in his claws again. He'll break my next pair of glasses, and the next, and the next because he has his sights set on me, Grandpa. And no García punch is gonna save me."

"When you come back from the optometrist tomorrow, we'll get even with Ozzy," my grandpa said.

"If you hit him to defend me, they'll call me a wimp."

"I won't hit him; I'm going to act as a mediator."

"A mediator?"

"That's something, Manolito, that there should have been in all the big wars: a mediator that accomplishes with words what can't be accomplished with fists and bombs."

I would've liked to warn my grandpa that with Ozzy the Bully, words go in one ear and out the other. Ozzy doesn't care about the teacher's words, his mom's words (she's always lecturing him), superheroes' words (he only watches cartoons), or the words of kids like me. He only wants to play "pulverizing you"—sometimes a "Captain America" version and other times a "Batman" version, but the outcome is always the same: pulverize you—well, more like pulverize *me*.

I told my grandpa I was going to sleep on his side of the bed the whole blessed night. It's just that I get scared sleeping without my glasses on. When I set out to have a day full of bad luck, I'm capable of tripping up even in my dreams; it's already happened to me more than once.

The next day, my dad and I went to the optometrist. Since neither one of us could see very well, we caught a taxi. It was really strange to go out with my dad in the morning on a school day; it's always my mom who goes with me everywhere.

We had a terrific time. Going to the optometrist is a whole lotta cool. I love how the guy asks what you see, and you tell him: "a *P* and now a *J* and now a *K*." It's the only time in your life when you get asked something and you don't mess it up if you give the wrong answer.

After the optometrist, we went to have breakfast in a café. I told my dad I wanted to sit on one of the bar stools, the ones that spin around. It was five pounds of cool. My dad let me order a shake, a chocolate croissant, and a doughnut. There weren't any other kids in the café; they must've been putting up with all the other Miss Asuncións in the worldwide world. I looked in the café's mirror to see the hairdo I'd given myself that morning—it had the part on the side and a doo-wop wave like Superman's—and I thought, "Maybe everyone here doesn't think I'm a kid; maybe they think that, instead of a ten-year-old boy, I'm eighteen. Maybe they think my dad and I are friends, or cousins. Of course, when I put my feet on the ground, they'll discover my real height. . . ."

The waiter came up to my dad and said, "It looks like the boy's hungry." Then he said to me, "If you keep eating like that, you're gonna be taller than your dad."

Some waiters know everything. Or maybe my face is an open book. As my mom always says—I can't fool anyone.

My dad let me eat another pastry, then he spun me around a few times on the stool, and he promised that one day he'd take me on a long trip in his truck (a.k.a. Manolito). As you can see, he didn't hold a grudge against me for breaking his glasses. So I thought that I shouldn't hold a grudge against Ozzy, either—but I did, and a lot. I held the biggest grudge in the world right then. I take after my mom that way: she's really spiteful, too, when she puts her mind to it.

Everything was really strange that day. My dad ate lunch at home as if it were Sunday. The only thing that stayed the same was my mom, who made peas.

My grandpa always asks us, "Where are we up to in peas?"

"We're up to our knees!" the Bozo and I scream with all our might.

In the afternoon, my grandpa took me to school, like every afternoon, and my parents stayed home and took a nap— what nerve. The moment was approaching when my grandpa would act as a mediator in our Big War. Ozzy the Bully and his grandpa were at the door of the school. My grandpa took me by the hand, and we walked toward them. I was getting ready to take another punch. At least my glasses couldn't get broken this time; they were still being fixed at the optometrist's.

My grandpa said to Ozzy's grandpa, "Look what happened to my grandson's eye when he got punched."

"What an animal!" said Ozzy's grandpa. Ozzy looked away as if the conversation had nothing to do with him.

"And you couldn't defend yourself, Manolito?" asked Ozzy's grandpa.

"Well, the other kid was more of a bully," answered my grandpa, "and he also broke my grandson's glasses."

"And glasses cost so much," said Ozzy's grandpa. "If my Ozzy had been with him, he would've given that punk what he deserves. Right, Ozzy?"

Ozzy was really red. He was looking at the ground, but he nodded his head yes.

My grandpa got up really close to Ozzy and finished the conversation by saying, "That's what I hope happens the next time. That bully can count on one thing for sure: if this happens again, all of us will give him a good knuckle sandwich. That's the only way to teach cowards who only dare to fight the weakest kids. And now, Manolito, go to class with Ozzy. With him, you don't have to be scared. He'll defend you from anyone. If you're with Ozzy, I won't be worried."

It was incredible. My grandpa deserved the Nobel Peace Prize. Ozzy and I went into school without saying anything.

In class, Ozzy passed me a note. It said:

Do you think your gramfather will tell my gramfather that it was me who broke your glasses?

I answered him with another note:

I don't know. I don't know if my graNDfather will tell your graNDfather that you're the guilty one.

I don't think Ozzy got the hint about his spelling; he's a real animal, in every sense of the word. I was sure that my grandpa hadn't told on him, but I wanted the bully to sweat it out awhile.

When we left school, our two grandfathers were waiting for us. I ran toward them, but since I wasn't wearing my glasses, I tripped. Well, to tell you the truthful truth, I have to admit that I usually trip with or without my glasses, every way possible.

Then something unbelievable happened: Ozzy the

Bully stooped down and helped me pick up my wallet and sweater. I would've liked to have taken a picture of the toughest guy on the planet picking up my stuff. It's not something that happens every day.

When he stood up again, Ozzy said, "He definitely told him."

In other words, the bully was afraid. I think it was one of the happiest days of my life on the Blue Planet. But no, my Grandpa Nicolás hadn't let the cat out of the bag; he's not like that. Ozzy realized it right away because his grandfather was the same with him as always. The four of us

walked the route together, the two grandfathers and two grandsons—we'd never walked down the street together before. Ozzy only came near me once to kick me. It was the only close moment we'd ever had. (That and the time he broke my glasses.)

Ozzy broke the infernal ice between us: "We don't have any other choice but to be friends."

"Well, yeah, you already heard what my grandpa said

would happen to you if you touch me again."

Right then, Big Ears showed up. He looked at us spellbound. He couldn't believe Ozzy the Bully and I were walking down the street like two normal guys.

"What are you lookin' at, dimwit?" Ozzy asked very politely.

Big Ears was about to run away, but I stopped him and told Ozzy, "If you're my friend, you'll have to be his friend, too. Answer: yes or no?"

Those were seconds of great atmospheric tension. Ozzy finally answered "yes." What could he do? He didn't have any choice. But he also set his conditions: "You, swear on your father that you'll never call me Captain Lush again in your life."

I swore on my father, my mother, the Bozo, my grandpa, but most of all I swore to myself. I knew that if I uttered that name again, my life would be at risk. Anyway, since nobody else can get inside my brain, I can still call him that mentally for centuries and centuries: *Captain Lush*!

That night I had to sleep without my glasses and on my grandpa's side again. I felt pretty important; I felt like the founder of my own crew, like the founder of a country (of the United States, just to mention the biggest country that occurs to me). Very few people have founded a crew in their lives, and I was one of them. I deserved a statue in Hangman's Park, a statue with a plaque that would say:

> *To Manolito Four-Eyes*
> *Illustrious child, founder of the crew that*
> *played on the very ground you're stepping on.*

It's true that none of the members of the crew were very sure about wanting to belong to it, but as my grandpa says, "You can't please everyone."

5

An Original Sin

If I went to Religion class, I'd have to confess to the priest an original sin I committed the other day. But since I only go to Ethics class, I'm only going to tell *you* (and half of Spain) cuz I like you. Plus, I'm not the type to go around the streets asking, "Excuse me, listen, are you a priest? Do you want me to confess a pretty original sin?"

People would take me for a nut. Some people would say, "C'mon, get outta town, clown," and others would take off petrified. My mom signed me up for Ethics to see if I would learn some manners, which she said I could sure use: "You could at least make less noise when you eat, Son."

My grandpa sure makes noise when he eats, but since the teeth he wears aren't his (they're from Wal-Mart), everyone forgives him. Anyway, the only thing Miss Asunción teaches us in Ethics is to repeat a thousand times that if we keep being the bunch of animals that we are, we'll end up delinquents. But that's nothing new; she tells us that all the time, even in Math; even in my dreams that ruthless woman is saying it.

Now, back to the pretty original sin (and not just because it's mine) that I committed the other day. I'm going to tell you this from the beginning of time:

The other day my grandpa came to pick me up from school. Everything was the same as usual. He gave me, with his shaky hand, a crispy, crunchy baguette with Cabrales blue cheese, and I went and said, "Grandpa, how many times do I have to tell you that the smell of Cabrales cheese reminds me of the locker room in my school?"

My grandpa answered, "No, no, spaceshot. You fell for it, nitwit. The Cabrales is for me, and yours is the baguette with butter."

My grandpa has pulled this joke on me, no exaggeration, about one hundred fifty thousand five hundred and twenty-five times; but he doesn't remember because of his bad prostate, so I have to make believe the joke is brand-new and say, "Thank God, Grandpa. For a minute there, I thought I'd have to swallow the Cabrales."

He's thrilled that I laugh over a joke that we play every

other day—or, as my mom says, on alternate days. Like I said, everything was the same as usual on that cold, charcoal-gray winter afternoon.

My grandpa asked me, "Your teacher wouldn't be that young girl with the red miniskirt?"

And I answered, "No, Grandpa, my teacher is that old and ruthless lady with the long black skirt."

"What bad luck, Manolito. My condolences."

Things were still going as usual: my grandpa never loses the hope that my teacher could be that young girl in the miniskirt and—with the excuse of "How's my grandson doing in Math?"—he might invite her to have a coffee and anchovies (which is what my grandpa likes to eat when he cashes his pension check). My grandpa never loses hope with the ladies. He always says I take after him that way. It's true: look at how the One-and-Only Susana shoots me down dead, and it's nothing; I go back to her like flies to manure. And by that, I don't mean that I'm a fly.

Almost every afternoon my grandpa and I say the same things; we laugh at the same things, and we eat the same snacks. And whose fault is that? Our own—because we like the same things, and whoever doesn't like it, they can go to Norway, like my uncle Nicolás did.

In that very non-crucial moment in our lives, one of the shady guys that hang around my neighborhood came up and told my grandpa to give him a Euro.

And my grandpa threw back: "Over my dead body am I giving you a Euro." (That's about $1.40, but my grandpa has a firm mind about these things.)

So, without beating around the bush, the guy took out a very large knife.

"Now you're gonna give me everything you have on you," he said.

My grandpa, who changes his mind once you insist with a knife, said, "You got it. Manolito, give this kind gentleman the money."

I was carrying it. My mom sticks money in my pocket every day so that I can buy a scratch ticket. (In my home,

we'd all like to be instant millionaires and forget we've ever known you. There has to be something to prove we're from the same family.)

I took out coin after coin. My mom gives it to me in coins so that she can get rid of the change in her purse. The mugger started to have a coronary. No matter how good a mugger is, there comes a moment in a mugger's life when he (or she, of course) gets tired of waiting and has other things to do. Since I was so nervous, I dropped the coins all on the ground. When the guy bent down to pick them up and take-off-without-looking-back, I could see the knife up close and I read the engraving:

SOUVENIR FROM MOTA DEL CUERVO

And, just to start up a topic of conversation in that moment of high atmospheric tension, I said, "That knife is from my grandpa's village."

And my grandpa continued the conversation by asking, "And why do you have a knife from Mota del Cuervo? And when were you there? And what's your mother's name? And what's your blood type? And what color is your underwear . . . ?" My grandpa always gets so annoying when he meets someone else from Mota del Cuervo.

Our mugger said yes, he's from Mota del Cuervo and told us his mother's name. (The name of the mugger's mother, not the name of my grandpa's mother; she died about a century ago, and it's not like we're about to start crying for all the people who died on planet Earth.) The mugger's mother is Joaquina, and my grandpa knew her.

"Joaquina, alias the Stump?" my grandpa asked nicely.

The mugger told him not even to think about telling his mother he robbed us because she could get worried, and it was a dirty mugger lie to boot. But my grandpa said that if the guy kept mugging people in my neighborhood, he was going to call the Stump, who was a saint; and he said he'd call the police so they could arrest the guy in handcuffs, and people on the street would point at him, saying, "That's the thug who dared to stick up Nicolás Moreno and Manolito Four-Eyes."

To wrap it up, my grandpa let loose with this: "And give me that knife. I don't want my village's name tarnished by your misdeeds, creep."

That's what my grandpa said, although the truth is, our creepy mugger behaved pretty well—he gave my grandpa the SOUVENIR FROM MOTA DEL CUERVO knife, and he gave us back our money "religiously," as my mom says.

I thought this impressive story ended there; you thought the same thing and so did the president of the United States. Well, the three of us got it wrong, because the most interesting part was yet to come.

☞

Two days later, Miss Asunción said, "Get in line—we're going to the Prado Museum."

Don't go thinking this was a surprise. We knew a week ago we were going to the big art museum downtown, but we ran to the door as if we'd never seen a door in our lives.

My mom had made me a potato tortilla in a crispy, crunchy baguette; some breaded steaks; and a chocolate croissant (for dessert) to take to the Prado Museum. When I opened my snack on the bus, Ozzy said I was one heck of a cheeseball and that it looked like I was going camping and not to the Prado Museum. I got so mad that I said, "Want some?" and the dude ate up half the tortilla, but he didn't call me a cheeseball again. If my mom found out, she'd kill me; she says all the kids in the worldwide world eat my crispy, crunchy baguettes.

Just when we were having the best time—Big Ears had already puked twice, and we'd sung "Mr. Bus Driver doesn't smile! He doesn't smile, Mr. Bus Driver!" three times—we arrived at the Prado Museum. Miss Asunción said that if we behaved badly, we'd never go on a field trip again in all the years of our lives, unless it was to the jail in Carabanchel. Miss Asunción wanted to take us to see Velázquez's *Las Meninas*, which is a very famous painting; that's why my school is called Diego Velázquez.

I never got to see that painting. Instead, on the way there we saw one with three ladies who were pretty ancient. You could tell they were ancient because they all had, as my mom says, the body of a pigeon: tiny little lips and big ol' hips. And we ended up stuck there—Big Ears,

Ozzy, and I—in front of those pigeon ladies the whole time. But in that museum, you see one painting and you get an idea of all the rest. The thing is, they all look alike. The three ancient broads were nude and had such big ol' legs that if one of those ladies booted you with one of her big ol' legs, you and your whole crew'd be dead for the rest of your lives.

All of a sudden, Big Ears read the title, and it turned out the big ol' painting was called *Three Graceful Ladies*. Ozzy fell on the ground cracking up, and the next thing you knew, Big Ears and I fell down so as not to be left out. Ozzy took out a fat magic marker from his hoodie to write on the painting *Three Big Broads* and then the museum's security guard came running over and asked us about our teacher and practically took us handcuffed over to Miss Asunción. She was with the whole class looking at a painting of a family staring straight ahead, like the video we have of the Bozo's baptism. When she saw us, even the lenses of my glasses began trembling.

But then something happened that changed the course of our lives completely. I saw a guy move up next to Miss Asunción. The guy . . . the guy . . . was the same one who tried to stick up my grandpa and me!

Before the security guard could mercilessly rat us out, I threw myself into the arms of Miss Asunción—I never thought I'd stoop so low—and I said, "Miss Asunción, the infamous mugger from Mota del Cuervo is trying to take your purse, and not only is he a mugger, he's the son of Joaquina the Stump!"

So Miss Asunción complained to the security guard about the lack of protection in the museum. As for me, Miss Asunción gave me a kiss on the cheek and told me I could sit in the front seat of the bus with her as a badge of honor (or some kind of badge, I don't remember).

Before we left the museum, we all went to the bathroom, which is what we do whenever they take us anywhere. And there was the mugger again! He grabbed my arm and said, "Look, Four-Eyes"—I can't figure out how he knew my nickname—"I came from Mota del Cuervo to Madrid because no one knows me in this city, and it turns out you're gonna screw up my business every day."

I told him that I didn't mean any harm and that I had accused him so they wouldn't accuse me. To make him stop squeezing my arm, I told him about a place where he could go around mugging people with some elbow room, where he could pull out another knife from Mota del Cuervo without me or my grandpa interrupting when it's none of our business. He seemed grateful for that advice and let me go.

When I got on the bus late, Miss Asunción was waiting for me in the front seat. But for once in history, she didn't chew me out. I sat right in front of my classmates' noses, next to Our Teach . . . in my new role as Brown-nose Boy.

Manolito Four-Eyes

I was pretty happy for about three and a half minutes. Then I started to get as bored as a sheep: I heard Ozzy the Bully getting hoarse from singing "Big Ears doesn't have a wiener," and I was dying of jealousy.

Our Teach took advantage of the situation to point out all the monuments as we passed by, and I started thinking that Madrid was overrun by monuments. She was really happy to have a new brown-noser. But deep inside, I knew I'd committed an original sin, a sin I'd never be able to confess because I don't go to Religion class and I don't know a single priest: the place I told the Mota del Cuervo mugger to go sticking up people was the stoop of Miss Asunción's apartment.

Like I said in the beginning, it was a pretty original sin.

Since then, I've watched Miss Asunción every morning to see if she looks like she's been mugged. My grandpa told me not to worry—that the muggers from his village never get up before eleven o'clock in the morning, and by that time she is already in school crushing our brains. That is a relief because, I'll tell you one thing, I love when Our Teach is away—but I also love her.

6

Made for Each Other

Now I'm going to tell you a love story from the beginning of time.

One day my grandpa came to pick me up from karate. I take karate because I walk like a penguin, and my dad says karate can fix this; it has to be fixed because it looks pathetic to walk around all day like a penguin unless you *are* a penguin. (My feet are filthy, but not webbed, just to set the record straight.)

Anyway, my grandpa came to pick me up from karate, and he said to me, "Why isn't your great friend Big Ears coming with us today?"

"My great friend? My great dog," I answered, without

hiding a deep-rooted hatred.

I told my grandpa that while I was at karate, in order to stop walking like the penguin I never was, Big Ears took the One-and-Only Susana to his house to watch the Tasmanian Devil cartoon. Big Ears did that, even knowing that I'd asked the One-and-Only Susana out on the first day of school. What happened to me last year was that all the other kids started asking girls out before I did, like they were possessed. So I ended up being the last one to ask, and the only girl available was Jessica the Fat Fatty. She was my girlfriend for two days. The first day, to start up an interesting conversation, I asked her, "So why are you so fat?"

"Because I want to be an opera singer when I grow up," she answered.

The next day, that girl was just waiting to get back at me. The spiteful Jessica asked me, "So why do you wear glasses, Four-Eyes?"

"So Ozzy can break them."

And then we stopped talking to each other. This year Jessica isn't fat anymore, and a kid that she says is better looking than me asked her out. She says he's better looking because he doesn't wear glasses; but my grandpa told me that, after many years, girls begin to like guys with glasses because they usually have more money. So that good-looking kid will get a wake-up call in about fifty-five years.

Well, like I said an hour ago, the One-and-Only Susana Dirty Underpants went with Big Ears to watch the Tasmanian Devil. I told my grandpa that the One-and-Only Susana had no respect—that even though someone else had already asked her out, she'd go out with anyone who gave her anything. And that's why she's had forty thousand boyfriends and I've had one girlfriend, and it was only lip service, as my mom says. My grandpa told me it wasn't enough to ask a girl out—that you have to tell her how you feel; take her to Hangman's Park and tell her, "I like you in the morning, in the afternoon, and in the evening." Just like that, day after day after day, for all of eternity, here on Earth and in outer space. My grandpa says that every guy in the worldwide world has said that to a girl at some point in his life. I wasn't totally convinced, but my mom always tells me, "Don't try to be different."

The next day, I told the One-and-Only Susana that I wanted to see her after school in Hangman's Park to tell her something really important. She said that's the same time as the Tasmanian Devil; she doesn't miss the Tasmanian Devil for anything in the world, so I should tell her that really important thing to her face right then. She also said she wasn't going to Hangman's Park since one time she found a large knife on the ground there, and she gave it to her mother as a souvenir; and the kicker was her mother reacted like ivy (climbing up the walls), screaming, "You're not going out tomorrow, not tomorrow and not ever." From that very instant on, the One-and-Only Susana just went from house to house to have a snack and watch the Tasmanian Devil because there weren't any large knives lying around in people's houses, not unless the kid's father was a mugger from Mota del Cuervo.

So I invited the One-and-Only Susana to my house. All the better for me, since my house has heating and Hangman's Park doesn't. My mom put some cushions on the floor for us so we wouldn't get the couch dirty; after all, she bought it brand-new five years ago.

You see, the day before I had told my mom, "Tomorrow, the One-and-Only Susana Dirty Underpants is coming over for a snack."

My mom chewed me out; she told me that's the worst thing you can say about a girl, and the best thing to do with a girl's underpants is not to look at them and leave them in peace.

But picture this:

When the One-and-Only Susana came over, and she

hitched up her dress to sit on the couch—which is what she always does: hitch up her dress to sit anywhere—my mom was the first one to take a look. And she decided to put the cushions on the floor for us. Then she called me into the kitchen to give me the chocolate milks, and the lady said to me, real low, "What's the deal? Her mother doesn't give her a clean change of clothes every day?"

I had to explain that her mother did, but that the One-and-Only Susana's underwear was a case for the show *Unsolved Mysteries*. Her mother—who'd had to come in to talk with Miss Asunción—said that her daughter's underpants got covered in dirt even when she was wearing sweatpants, and scientists from all over the world needed to come to Spain to find out why underpants that left the house white in the morning ended up black by lunchtime. Why? No one can explain it. It's one of planet Earth's greatest enigmas.

I was giving my mom this explanation when she said, "All right, Manolito. Enough about the underpants. You get on a topic, and no one can get you off it. Go be with your friend."

My mom's like that: she'd like it if I answered all of her questions with a yes or a no, so she can turn around and talk on the phone to one of her friends. That's why she likes the Bozo better—he's one of those "on the down low" types. That's the kind of kid my mom likes; that's why she married my dad, because my dad speaks only three times a year: on New Year's Eve, on his birthday, and when the Real Madrid team wins a soccer match.

I went back to the cushions and the One-and-Only Susana, who told me that Big Ear's TV was cooler than mine because it was God-only-knows-how-many inches bigger and that she drank chocolate milk only with Cocoa Krispies. I asked my grandpa to go down to the store and buy Cocoa Krispies. I said that if he did me that favor, I'd remember it even after he died.

My grandpa went down the stairs, saying, "That little One-and-Only Susana has us all beat to a pulp."

When the Tasmanian Devil ended, the moment of the famous declaration had come: "Well . . . I wanted to tell you that . . . that I really like your headband."

That's the only thing I could come up with.

And she answered, "Well, I'm not gonna give it to you."

The truth is that I could've said something better, but

she didn't have to give me that answer, either. There was a pretty deadly silence between us.

After watching commercials awhile, she said, "Maybe you're a girl."

Now, that I didn't expect at all, so I had to explain, "No, what I like is seeing it in your hair, not mine."

And then the chick started laughing—she said she was imagining me with my glasses, my bangs (which are a bit stiff), and the headband. She insisted I put it on, and I said no, and she said yes.

I told her, "All right, I'll put it on, and then you're my girlfriend."

She said, "Okay, okay, okay."

She was obsessed with my putting on her headband. And I put it on because I always have to do whatever any-one tells me to do. I think nobody has ever laughed at someone as much as the One-and-Only Susana laughed at me that day. Her skirt got crumpled up from laughing so hard. The Bozo caught the laughing fit, and that one is always on the side of whoever's laughing the hardest. Then my mom came in to see "what on God's green Earth" all the racket was about. When she saw me with the head-band on, she said, "You're such a clown, Manolito."

And that was the kicker! After an hour and a half, the girl stopped pointing and laughing. Then she threw it in my face that she was getting bored, and the only thing that could stop the boredom was to play dress up and make up our faces. I had to grab, on the sly, some nightgowns from my mom's room and her makeup bag. The One-and-Only Susana said she was Aladdin's princess. She said I was Aladdin's genie and directed me to stand in my underwear with a bandanna on my head. The chick started rubbing the lamp, which was a crystal blue and red vase of my mom's, and asking for one wish after another and another:

"Now bring the Bozo to me. He's my son and he was kidnapped. Now kill the guy who's trying to invade the palace. Now give me more Cocoa Krispies. Now a glass of water . . ."

She had me frazzled, sweating, going from one room to another. Compared to me, Aladdin's genie lived like a prince. In the middle of it all, she went to rub the magic lamp, and she busted my mom's blue and red vase. I thought the same thing my mom always says when we break something: "I saw it coming from a mile away."

Luckily, my mom had to run out for something. If she'd been there, she would have given me the corresponding lecture in front of the One-and-Only Susana. Because if my mom wants to chew you out at any given moment of her life, she chews you out, even if it's in front of millions of television viewers. She doesn't hold back for anyone.

As we watched my grandpa pick up the pieces of the vase, the One-and-Only Susana said, "If you're my boyfriend, don't even think about telling your mom it was me who broke it."

After she said that, the One-and-Only Susana stuck a handful of Cocoa Krispies in her coat and marched out the front door.

Grandpa and I had to put the Bozo on the couch so he wouldn't get cut, but he managed to grab a piece of the vase off the floor and cut himself anyway. I had to wash him up myself since my grandpa's bad prostate makes him get dizzy at the sight of blood. The Bozo didn't stop crying, and to get him to quiet down, I had to give him my dad's shaving cream. Cans of foam always calm him down.

After a while, my mom came home. She doesn't work for the CIA—because the CIA doesn't know she exists—but I swear that my mom's a hundred thousand times better than James Bond and all his enemies. She stepped on the floor, and the floor went *crack* under her shoes. She looked right at the table, and she knew the vase had been broken. She looked at the couch, and she knew the Bozo had been lifted up there but had cut himself anyway. She smelled my dad's shaving cream in the air, and she knew the Bozo had used it all up. She looked at my grandpa, and she knew he was fed up. And then she looked at me, and when she saw me with my head scrunched down into the neck of my sweatshirt, she knew I was waiting for my corresponding lecture.

She breathed in to start her speech, but my grandpa interrupted her, "Don't say anything to the kiddo. I was the one who broke the vase. I gave the shaving cream to the Bozo, and I lifted him up on the couch."

So my mom began to chew out my grandpa, and my grandpa took advantage of the moment to go down and have a coffee in Stumbles, which is what he always does when he doesn't like the outlook at home.

Each night, I usually heat up my grandpa's feet, and he usually compensates me with ten cents in my piggy bank—but that night I told him I'd heat them up for free since he saved me from the electric chair.

My grandpa said that if I stuck with that girlfriend, I'd be the first child in the worldwide world to have a heart attack.

The next day at recess, the One-and-Only Susana ordered me to insult a boy in the fourth grade, bring her sand to make a castle, and play bubonic plague with her and three of her friends. Whoever gets the bubonic plague has to catch the rest of the players, and no one can touch the victim or even brush against him. The One-and-Only Susana ordered me to be the plague victim for the whole recess. I thought, "Bore galore." It was the most obnoxious recess of my life on this planet.

When we were going back to class, I told Big Ears, "Today you can invite the One-and-Only Susana to watch the Tasmanian Devil. I have karate."

My friend Big Ears is not known for being a great observer, but I don't know how this act of generosity on my part didn't seem strange to him.

I had a fantastic time in karate. My teacher told me that I had to put a gigantic giant from the fifth grade in a headlock. For a minute there, I thought my teacher had gone crazy or he wanted to do me in for good. My teacher explained the headlock to me. I always understand my karate teacher's theories; I even imagine them in my head. I can see myself pulling off some *Karate Kid*-type jumps at the edge of the Grand Canyon, but then everything gets screwed up in reality. I can't explain it. My grandpa says, "That's life."

Now, you're not gonna believe it, but I put the human boulder from the fifth grade in a headlock. It was like kicking a mountain: the guy didn't move from his spot. The bad part is that when I made my move, my glasses went flying through the air—even though my mom had tied them onto my brain with a rubber band. I had a fantastic time in karate, but I had an even better time when my mom said she couldn't care less if I walk like a penguin; I wasn't going back to karate because she wasn't going to pay for any more glasses this year.

That was the best news of the season. I was sick of fighting all the mountains in the school.

The next day, when I told Big Ears I'd never go back to karate unless Spain was invaded by Martians, he said, "Great! The One-and-Only Susana can go over to your house every afternoon. At my house yesterday, she broke the remote control. She was Aladdin's princess and I was her genie, but that rubbing the lamp bit was old news to her. She said she was going to order me around with the remote control. After two hours, I said I was sick of obeying her, and she threw the remote at my head. My mom asked, 'How about finding a less obnoxious girlfriend?'"

"Wait, the One-and-Only Susana's your girlfriend, too?"

We started arguing about who had betrayed who, but after a minute and a half, we realized it was ridiculous—the One-and-Only Susana has more boyfriends than there are boys in our school. She also has boyfriends at the school across the street, in her building, and in Navas del Marques, which is her mother's village. Almost all the guys in Spain are the One-and-Only Susana's boyfriends.

Big Ears and I talked about that the whole way home. We were like two great friends with the same problem—like, how in the movies at the end you see two friends walking off together into the cold and horrific fog. With how well we were getting along, I don't know how it all got messed up, but we began to argue again over who had more right to watch the Tasmanian Devil with the One-and-Only Susana.

It was pretty clear: neither one of us wanted to deal with the One-and-Only Susana, but we didn't want her to spend the afternoon with our best friend, either. In these terrible situations, my grandpa says, "People are just strange like that."

Well, we were just about to fight over something that neither of us wanted, when suddenly, without prior warning, we saw the One-and-Only Susana in Hangman's Park jumping on a bench—with a boy. We got closer. It was . . . Ozzy!

We watched them for a while. They were having a terrific time. They played book-bag launch kicks, they pushed each other to get the best swing, and then they flung themselves on the ground when they swung up really high. Ozzy took the One-and-Only Susana's headband and ran off. The One-and-Only Susana caught up, grabbed him by the hair, and spit on him. On Ozzy! On the biggest bully in my class, in my neighborhood, in all of Spain! Nobody had ever dared in their life to spit on Ozzy—you could really pay for that.

Big Ears and I held our breaths; he held his and I held mine. Our heartbeats were like drums announcing a terrifying war. What would happen next?

Well, nobody will ever believe it. You're not gonna believe it, but it went like this, I swear on my grandpa.

Big Ears said very soft and shaky, "He's gonna turn her face inside out."

But he and I, and the whole worldwide world, were wrong because Ozzy wiped off the spit and said, "Sorry, I was just playing. It was a joke. You didn't have to spit on me with so much saliva."

And after he said that, they just kept on playing, pushing each other and jumping like nuts. Big Ears and I turned around and left; first of all, because we were out of place there, and second, because we were afraid they'd ask us to play with them.

Now it clearly was ridiculous to fight over the One-and-Only Susana. We didn't say it, but I think we both thought it, and we both thought it was a relief that she liked Ozzy better, too.

That afternoon, I invited Big Ears to watch the Tasmanian Devil at my house. We had a fantastic time, eating bread and butter with chocolate milk and watching cartoons, the two of us stretched out on the couch. We both had our heads on the same end because Big Ears has smelly feet. The poor kid's not perfect.

My grandpa looked at us and said to my mom, "They're made for each other."

And for a minute, I didn't know if he was talking about Big Ears and me or the One-and-Only Susana and Ozzy the Bully, who might still be throwing dirt in each other's eyes in Hangman's Park.

They were made for each other, too. It must be love.

7

Paquito Medina Is Not from This Planet

I'm going to be grounded on Sunday, and Saturday, too. My mom will have me locked up mercilessly inside these four walls. I'll be worse off than a gorilla in the zoo; at least a gorilla can see people that come to look at him like g he's a monkey, but nobody comes to see me. I have to be satisfied with my cage mates: my grandpa and the Bozo.

When I get grounded, I get tough—like the bread my grandpa likes, the kind that's been in the bread box for two days. I get an upset stomach, too, because I get bored, and when I'm bored, I spend the whole afternoon back and forth from the minibar to the couch.

The minibar is a piece of furniture that my mom

bought for my dad because my dad always says, "Catalina, I'm a bar guy."

And having said that, he'd go down to Stumbles Bar.

My mom, who has a solution for everything, gave him a minibar last Father's Day, a cushioned bar with real imitation leather. You open it, and you see a mirror-filled interior; and if there are three bottles, for a minute there, you think there are sixteen. That's what scientists all over the world call "the phenomenon of multiplication."

After he unwrapped it, my mom said, "So you're a bar guy, right? Well, from now on, you don't need to go down to the bar; you have the bar at home."

At first, the minibar was sacred, and my mom put in only my dad's Fundador cognac, my grandpa's anisette, and a bottle of Bagpiper cider that was left over from Christmas. But since there's no space in our house for anything, the famous, sacred minibar turned into a supermarket.

"We don't have cockroaches in this house," my mom tells Our Nosy Neighbor Luisa. "We wouldn't mind, but the thing is, they don't fit."

My mom's got her little jokes, too. Don't go thinking

she's always in a stinky mood.

Anyway, first we put in the sacred bar some Cheetos, hazelnuts, and stuff my mom puts out for visitors (that the Bozo and I eat in fifty milliseconds). Then she kept going with the chocolate milk, the Cocoa Krispies left over from the One-and-Only Susana's visit, and the things my mom calls our "gross snacks." Last month, she began storing the bathroom-cleaning products in there. That's so the Bozo won't eat them, since one of the Bozo's vices is bleach: the little drunk has already tried it twice.

So when I'm grounded, I spend the afternoon going back and forth from the minibar. I grab a handful of Cheetos, another of Cocoa Krispies, and another of caramel-coated almonds. When they ground me for more than one day, I'm about to explode. I get the classic blockage in my large intestine, and my mom tells the doctor, "This boy has gotten so stuffed, he can't move the ball of food up above or down below."

When my mom says "up above," she's referring to my mouth, and when she says "down below," she's referring to my rear end. My mom talks to the doctor about my rear end as if it were a subject that should interest him. When my mom says that "down below" bit, I don't know where to look. I think the doctor gets embarrassed, too. I'm not surprised. If I were a doctor giving a checkup to a kid I hardly knew, I wouldn't want his mother talking to me about his rear end.

In any case, there are times when I don't end up with

an upset stomach, but I can guarantee you that being grounded turns me into the biggest royal pain in my neighborhood and the world.

Now I'm going to tell you the story of my terrible grounding from the beginning of time:

There once was a marvelous boy who lived in Carabanchel, a real muscleman and really smart—there wasn't anyone like him. His name was Manolito Four-Eyes, and I don't know if you've figured it out, but that magnificent boy was me. And this kid, in a category by himself, got up one terrible Monday—last Monday—and thought, "Today I have an exam in Environmental Science, and I don't have a friggin' clue."

That boy—*me*—called to his mom and said, "Mother dearest, I think my fever's getting worse by the minute."

And the boy's mother—*mine*—touched my forehead and answered me with cruel indifference, "Manolito, get dressed or you'll be late."

"And what if I'm at school, and my fever goes up to a hundred and two and I'm sweating like a madman? Don't you think it's better to be safe than sorry?" I asked, since I never lose hope that someday I'll fool my mom.

"I'll make you sweat if you don't get up right now."

There was nothing I could do. When my mom gets like that, I realize she's not anything like the mothers in songs and poems—those mothers must live in America, in condos with two floors.

I went to school, and I sat at the desk as if I were sitting

in the electric chair. I told Big Ears, who sits next to me (and is my great friend even though sometimes he's *still* a dog traitor), "I'm planning on copying off you because I have N.F.C."

We said N.F.C. ever since the day we said "No friggin' clue" and Miss Asunción heard us; we decided it was better not to utter the word "friggin'" inside the school walls.

Big Ears answered, "Well, we'll have to copy off the kid in front of us because I have N.F.C. too."

The truth is that copying off Big Ears is ridiculous. He never writes anything on exams, and if he does, it's because he copied it off me.

Before Our Teach came in, we took a poll: the kids in the front didn't know anything and neither did the ones in the back, or the ones on the ceiling. That morning the worldwide world had N.F.C.

Our only hope was Paquito Medina.

Paquito Medina was new this year. He didn't come on the first day of class; he came a month later. Miss Asunción had warned us, "A new boy is coming tomorrow. His name is Paquito Medina, and don't ask him about his father, because he doesn't have one.

We were amazed by what Our Teach had said. After half a minute, Ozzy dared to ask, "And why doesn't he have one?"

"Because he died." Miss Asunción wasn't one for giving a lot of explanations.

"A long time ago?" asked Oscar Mayer. (He's named Oscar; we added on the Mayer bit.)

"Two months ago."

"Two months ago!" we all exclaimed in unison, as if we'd been practicing it for twenty-seven days.

"And why did he die? Was he really old?" asked Arturo Roman, who's always out in left field, according to Our Teach.

"How could he have been old if he was Paquito Medina's father?" said the One-and-Only Susana.

"What, you know Paquito Medina?" asked Ozzy. Sometimes he sounds really dumb.

"I've never seen him in my life," answered the One-and-Only Susana, who can be very sarcastic.

"He must've died from an incurable disease," I said. I always think the worst.

"He died from a heart attack." Another big explanation from Our Teach.

"And was he alone when he had the heart attack?"

asked Big Ears, who wants to know everything down to the last detail.

"I don't know. Let's start class."

"A friend of my dad's had a heart attack. They took him to the hospital dead, and in the hospital they brought him back to life with some electrodes they brought from the United States," I said—because it's absolutely true.

"Maybe they used up all the electrodes bringing your dad's friend back to life, and they didn't have time to go to the United States for more to save Paquito Medina's dad," said a kid in the back.

"Manolito's dad's friend has some nerve," said Jessica, who's not fat anymore.

"Well, your dad's friend has some nerve!" I yelled back at her.

Then other kids said that my dad's friend had some nerve, and others defended us: my dad's friend, my dad, and me.

Miss Asunción banged her fist down, but we kept yelling. On the third bang we shut up. It's always like that—it's mathematical.

"That's enough. I just want you to behave and for no one to ask about his father."

"Why?" asked Arturo Roman.

Miss Asunción kicked him out of class—and after that, it didn't occur to anyone to ask about Paquito Medina. We're pains, but we're not stupid.

Elvira Lindo

The next day Paquito Medina showed up at school. Our Teach sat him in the front row. We watched him closely for three days and thought about him for three nights. On the fourth day at recess, Paquito Medina showed us a pin with the symbol of the Rayo Vallecano soccer team, and he told us, "I'm a Rayo Vallecano fan like my dad."

"Did your dad die?" I asked him, without making a big deal of the question that we all had in our heads but weren't supposed to ask.

"Yeah. Before now we lived in Vallecas, where Rayo Vallecano rules. But when my dad died, my mom wanted us to move to a different neighborhood."

We spent the entire recess asking him for all the details. After all, he was the first friend we had without a father. After we found out all the stuff from his life before, almost nobody talked about that again—except to try to get Paquito Medina to stop following Rayo Vallecano and become a Real Madrid fan, since they're obviously the best soccer team in Madrid. Plus, Paquito Medina became known pretty fast for other things besides his father's death. It turned out that Paquito Medina is a golden boy.

As Miss Asunción says, "Paquito Medina should be in a contest." When Our Teach says that, she's not referring to any old contest on TV, but the Nobel Prize or a contest like that.

Paquito Medina is different from all the other normal

kids—he's always clean. Paquito Medina's fingernails are fit for an exhibition; his teeth never have bits of chocolate croissant stuck in them; Paquito Medina's notebooks look like textbooks.

The truth is, Paquito Medina deserves the Nobel Peace Prize.

And the other truth is that when you meet such a bright kid, it eats away at your morale. Deep down we all had the hope that once he wasn't the new kid anymore and became an old one like us, Paquito Medina would fail at something: in gymnastics, for example.

But not even that. Paquito goes out to the school yard wearing a navy blue sweat suit and sneakers that say "Rayo Vallecano" and jumps over the horse as if he were an Olympian. Paquito Medina never insults anybody; he doesn't fight Ozzy, and he never kicks other kids' book bags.

Paquito Medina isn't like us.

Big Ears says that Paquito Medina is a Martian put here in our school by other Martians to drive us crazy with envy, and that once he's driven us crazy, he'll go to other schools, and others, and others. And on and on, until all the children in the worldwide world are annihilated by Paquito Medina, that strange being from another planet.

Unmistakable proof that Paquito Medina is a Martian was unveiled to us one day in the locker room—we found out that he has two belly buttons, a smaller one next to the normal one that we Earthlings have. My theory is that Paquito Medina comes from a planet where women are Siamese twins and babies are attached to their mothers by two umbilical cords. In the locker room, we asked him a thousand five hundred questions about his extra belly button, but Paquito Medina wouldn't answer. He only said, "I was born with it."

That's the proof that Paquito Medina isn't from this planet.

I don't know if you remember, but a while ago I told you how one day I went to class with N.F.C. about a test on Environmental Science. I also told you that everyone in my whole class had a blank mind, like mine. So we asked Paquito Medina if he would mind us copying off him—because once you find yourself in vital necessity of copying off someone, you don't care if he's from planet Earth or another planet; when it comes right down to it, we all rotate around the Sun.

Paquito Medina got really happy when we asked him that small favor. That's more proof that Paquito Medina is an extraterrestrial. I let someone copy if they pay, but not a whole class—gimme a break.

Right off, Miss Asunción asked us a ruthless question about liquid, solid, and gaseous states. We all looked at her with hate in our eyes. I wouldn't wish a question like that on my worst enemy.

But Paquito Medina started to write, letting the kid behind him copy; and the kid behind him did the same and the one behind him; and so on until Big Ears and me (we are into sitting in the back seats).

I was excited. It's moments like those when you think that World Peace is possible: that human beings can form a great chain of friendship.

I gave my exam to Ozzy the Bully to copy (he sits even farther back); but Ozzy, who's a separatist, said, "I don't have to copy off Paquito Medina. I brought my cheat sheet from home."

Then Ozzy took his cheat sheet out of his nose. He balls it up into a diminutive roll and sticks it up there— even though one time, his mom had to take him to the emergency room because the cheat sheet had gone creeping up through his nostrils and was about to destroy his brain.

The next day we were all waiting for the grade on our test. I pictured Miss Asunción saying, "Manolito García Moreno, a big whopping one hundred."

I pictured going home with my test, and my mom telling Our Nosy Neighbor Luisa, "My Manolito got a big whopping one hundred."

But it didn't go like that—real life never matches my mental projections.

Miss Asunción came to class and, instead of handing out hundreds, she handed out letters. No one knew why. There were ten of us who got envelopes: me, Big Ears, the One-and-Only Susana, Arturo Roman, Jessica the ex-Fat Fatty, Paquito Medina, and four others you don't know.

Finally, Our Teach said, "You don't even know how to cheat."

She had snagged us. Paquito Medina had made a deadly error—he confused the question; instead of writing about liquid and gaseous states, he wrote about the layers of the atmosphere (you know, the stratosphere, among others).

Paquito Medina made a mistake, and the rest of us were bad cheaters. Miss Asunción said so. She wanted our parents to find out that when it comes to not knowing, we don't even know how to cheat. For the first time, she even got mad at Paquito Medina. According to Miss Asunción, letting people copy off you is cheating, too, and "such a bright child" making a mistake on a question is unforgivable. Paquito Medina had lost points. The Swedish Academy wouldn't be awarding him the Nobel Prize this year.

The funniest thing is that Ozzy passed. Sometim[es] gives you surprises as unpleasant as that one. Thank G[od] he only got a sixty. Ozzy says his boogers got in the way [of] the letters. Gimme a break.

Big Ears and I headed home with the letter in our book bags. There are times when letters are as heavy as pure steel. Big Ears wasn't as scared as I was; since his mom is divorced and feels guilty about whatever Big Ears does bad, she almost never chews him out. So for Big Ears, zeros go in one ear and out the other. But nobody has pity or compassion for me. I could already hear the lecture from my mom. It was a bad one. At least my dad gets home so late at night and so tired, he doesn't feel like lecturing. That's why I like that my dad's a truck driver. If he worked in an office, like the One-and-Only Susana's dad, he'd come home at five in the afternoon with enough energy to chew out a regiment. In any case, I get enough and then some from my mom.

Paquito Medina caught up to Big Ears and me. He was as cool as a cucumber.

"Miss Asunción gave me an envelope, too." He held it up as if it were a diploma.

"What, am I the only one who gets chewed out at home?" I walked away, angrily stomping the ground. I was sick and tired of my friends.

Paquito Medina ran to catch up to me. "Manolito!

I'm gonna get chewed out, too."

"I don't believe it." How was I supposed to believe a kid who says he's gonna get chewed out without batting an eye?

"I swear on my father."

But if he was swearing on his father, then it really was believable. Anyway, Paquito Medina always was weird.

"And you don't care if you get chewed out?" I asked.

"No, I do care." He got really serious. "It's not like I get chewed out a lot, because I always behave. I don't know how I do it, but I always behave."

"It's the opposite with me," I said. "I don't know how I do it, but I always misbehave."

"And I'm sick of it," said Paquito Medina.

"I'm sick of it, too."

"If you sit behind me some day, I'll let you copy off me," he promised.

"Make sure it's a day that you don't mess up the question, if you don't mind."

And he said no, he didn't mind. Then Paquito Medina said something else that I plan on remembering as long as I'm alive:

"When something bad happens to you, you have to think that you'll get over it, even though you don't believe it. You'll get over it, and someday you'll remember it as if it happened to another person."

"And how do you know that?" I asked.

"Because my dad told me once."

I tried to think about that, right when my mom was opening the letter from school. I thought, "This thing that's happening to me now—in three months, it won't matter; and in three years, it will seem like it happened to another person." I tried to keep thinking that when I saw the look in my mom's eyes after she read the letter. But I couldn't think it when she chewed me out, when she gave me the worldwide famous lecture, and when she grounded me for this weekend.

Now I can only think about two days of being locked in—worse than a gorilla in the zoo, tough as bread, sick and tired of eating Cheetos. And I also think about how Paquito Medina is obviously not a being from this planet. I don't know if he's from Mars or Venus or Jupiter. Wherever they may be, the inhabitants of his planet are obviously better people than the ones from mine.

8

I Don't Know Why I Did It

The idea occurred to me when Big Ears and I were on the way home.

We were playing the chain-words game. The One-and-Only Susana says it's a pretty dopey game, but if we had to listen to that girl, we wouldn't play anything.

She always says, "That game's pretty dopey."

"Then go make one up yourself. Gimme a break," I'd said to her a few days before, after school, when she had me fed up to my very eyeteeth.

Why'd I have to go and say anything at all? Her game was for the four of us—me, Big Ears, Ozzy, and her—to stand in the middle of the street until a car came, and at the last minute, start running. We'd go in pairs, and the winners would be the pair who stayed the longest, holding hands and blocking the street. The people in the cars gestured with their hands out the window and beeped when they saw that Ozzy the Bully and the One-and-Only Susana weren't moving away. I swallowed a lot of saliva, and my heart moved up to my throat. Big Ears' ears looked like two tomatoes. (You see, his ears change color when danger lurks. Scientists from all over the world have tried to find an explanation, and they haven't yet. My grandpa says it's because science doesn't have the answer for everything.)

The moment came when Big Ears and I went into the middle of the street, holding hands. All of a sudden, we saw a bus approaching mercilessly. Big Ears and I got the famous death cackle, a laugh you get when you're dying in the North Pole. Big Ears let go of my hand and sprinted over to the sidewalk.

Ozzy shouted, "Check out how brave that dude is!"

That dude was me, Manolito Four-Eyes. A bus couldn't take me out—not a bus; not even a jumbo jet could take me out—because I, with the power of my mind, went and stopped that four-wheeled beast. You wouldn't believe how surprised I was when I saw the bus stopping. Imagining that your mind has superpowers is one thing, and really having them is a whole other story. The bus stopped short (or maybe it was long?), and my friends applauded me. I saw the door of the bus open, and I thought, "Now the driver's going to ask me, 'How did you do it, Manolito? How were you able to seize control of the bus with the power of your mind?'"

But right off the bat, I realized that the driver would never ask me that. The driver wasn't a stranger—he was Mr. Solis, the school bus driver, and I knew he wasn't going to congratulate me on the power of my mind.

Mr. Solis came running off the bus and grabbed me by the coat to take me to the principal. Mr. Solis asked me if

I realized that I could've killed myself and killed him. My friends had stopped applauding and had left the sidewalk—the truth was, they'd disappeared. Mr. Solis yelled at me so hard that a little pellet of his saliva stuck to the lens of my glasses. Some cars that were behind his bus honked because they wanted to go by. Mr. Solis had to get back into the bus. He told me that I was saved by the skin of my teeth this time, and to go away, the farther the better.

So I went home alone with Mr. Solis's little pellet of saliva on my right lens. There are times in your life when you're not up for cleaning off a little spit.

That afternoon I didn't want a snack, and I almost didn't have dinner.

My mom said, "Something's wrong with this one."

I had to hide it because I didn't want my mom to find out that her son was much worse than she ever imagined.

That night I dreamed that Mr. Solis and I were dead in two open caskets, one right next to the other. I didn't mind being in that coffin; what I did mind was that no one had bothered to wipe off Mr. Solis's famous little pellet of saliva, and I couldn't see who had attended my funeral.

I woke up sweating, the way actors in movies wake up, and I woke up my grandpa to tell him what had happened to me. My grandpa said I didn't always have to do what my friends told me to do, that being brave doesn't mean doing what bullies want you to do, and that if Ozzy the Bully and the One-and-Only Susana were as brave as they say, they would've stuck around to defend a friend.

In other words, my grandpa was saying that Mr. Solis was right. It was the first time in my life that my grandpa took someone else's side. So I started crying because I felt pretty much alone on the planet Earth. But then my grandpa said that since he was sure I wasn't going to do something so ridiculous again, from now on we'd never think about it; and when all is said and done, anyone can make a mistake, especially when they're awake—so go to sleep.

Well, as I said back at the beginning, Big Ears and I were on our way home a few days after that terrible scene, playing chain words.

He'd say, "Bellhop."

And I'd answer, "Hopscotch."

As you can see, it's a much-less dangerous game than the kind that the One-and-Only Susana and Ozzy like. The only bad thing about it is that we always end in a tie because someone says: "Holdup."

"Uphold," the other answers.

"Holdup."

"Uphold!"

And so on, until the end of time—or until we say good-bye and each go our own way because by then we're sick and tired of each other.

We had finished the famous chain-words game, tied

up as usual, when the idea hit me for what I was going to do next. I nodded good-bye to Big Ears and took off running to my stoop. There, I opened my book bag, trembling with excitement, and I took out my three markers—fat markers that Martin from the fish shop gave us for Christmas that say **Happy Holidays! Martin Fish Shop** on the sides. (My mom, who always has to make everything difficult, said, "The customers would be much happier if he gave us a pound of shrimp.")

I took the caps off the mega-markers and began to walk up the stairs, pressing the tips against the wall. "How cool," I thought. I made three stripes: a red one, a blue one, and a black one. I tried to keep them very straight so they'd look like bullfighting spears. Not for nothing—it was coming out extraordinary. I made my fantastic bullfighting spears up to the third floor. Why did I go up to the third? Because I live on the third, as everyone in Spain knows.

My mom opened the door and looked at my hands, as she always does when I come in. My mom can look at your hands and know where you've been, at what time, and sometimes, even who was there with you. One time, my grandpa and I came home a little late. My mom took my hands, smelled them, and said to my grandpa, "You must think it's great to feed the boy shrimp. Now I'll eat lunch myself."

I'm telling you, my mom doesn't work for the CIA because the Americans haven't given her the chance, but she's a top-notch spy.

I was saying how she looked at my hands and saw them full of marker stains. She got paler than a sheet when

she spotted my fantastic bullfighting spears in the hall. She followed the trail down the stairs. And the Bozo followed her, tracing the colored lines with his finger. I think they got all the way to the front door. Then I heard them coming back up, very slowly. When my mom does something very slowly, it's because the Third World War is about to break out. When she got to the second floor, I started to cry, to see if I could avoid the explosion. I cried softly—something told me I should save my supply of tears for the next five hours.

My intuition hadn't failed me, friends. When my mom returned to the third floor, she gave me the corresponding lecture. My mom didn't get on the payroll for *Lethal Weapon 10* because there's no justice in this world, but my mom is a hundred times better than any cop. When she began the lecture, I thought, "Well, what a stupid lecture." But ten minutes into it, I felt all hot and embarrassed. If someone had put an egg on the nape of my neck right then, the egg would've fried. 'Nuff said. Even so, I'd choose a short lecture at the top of her lungs a thousand times over a long one. When my mom finds a good reason to chew you out for an hour, you're done for. The bore galore can last for weeks, sometimes months, even years.

That day, the issue at hand didn't have a very good outlook. My mom said, "This boy'll be the death of me. He drew with markers all over the stairwell that was just painted. And the kicker is, we can't hide that it was him, because this pip-squeak stopped the stripes right at our door. The neighbors will make us pay for the paint. We'll lose all our money. . . ."

My mom kept talking and talking and talking, but I wasn't listening to her anymore. The tears that fell from my eyes were now from shame. I pictured myself and my whole family on the street, freezing to death, with holes in our shirts, begging for charity and a crispy, crunchy baguette with peanut butter for a snack—like that family we saw one day in the Puerta del Sol who sang to earn spare change. My grandpa gave them a Euro to keep them quiet for a while because, personally, he couldn't stand their singing. People applauded my grandpa's incredible idea since the truth is, that family sang worse than all the families I've met in my life. My grandpa says that family now earns money by going to parks with a sign that reads:

If you don't give us your spare change, we'll sing.
(We have a flute and a four-stringed guitar.)

I bet it's really working out for them, and people fill up their hat with gold coins. My grandpa is out of this world at fixing people's lives. He's like Superman, but with fewer powers. The Bozo and I call him Superprostate.

My mom was still going: "Pretty soon the neighbors will come over to say, 'You should tie your Manolito's hands together' and 'Who is gonna pay to fix this?' And then at night your dad will come home and tell me, 'It's your fault for giving him the markers' and 'You explain to me how we're gonna pay for this extra expense.'"

Suddenly, my grandpa got up from his chair as if he were in the House of Representatives, raised his hand like he was going to say something important, and announced, "Don't worry, because . . . I have to go to the bathroom a minute."

It's not that we would've been worried that he was going to the bathroom; it's just that sometimes he gets the urge to go, and it has to interrupt the best statements of his life.

When he came back, he continued, "Don't worry, because Grandpa Nicolás is going to take care of this."

The Bozo clapped. To him, everything in life is really simple. I was the same way when I was little.

"Catalina," my grandpa went on in his House of Representatives voice, "not another word."

I guess it worked, because my mom went to clean up the kitchen. Once she was gone, my grandpa asked me in a really mysterious way about the markers. I got my book bag and gave them to him. He winked at me and walked out the door without another word.

I sat still on the couch, but curiosity wouldn't let me live even another second on the global Earth. I went out the door, just as sneakily as my grandpa had a few minutes before. When I saw what I saw, I couldn't believe it. You wouldn't have, either.

My grandpa was drawing three more stripes with the markers—from the third floor to the fourth!

I walked up to him very slowly and said softly, "Grandpa."

"Manolito, you almost scared me to death," he said.

The two of us were speaking as softly as when we're in bed.

"What are you doing, Grandpa?"

"I'm drawing the stripes up to the fourth floor, so nobody can blame you for sure. They'll have to blame the guy on the fourth floor, too. No matter how much they accuse you, you deny it all. Now, go home."

Superprostate had done it again!

I went back into my apartment, and five minutes later, we heard screams in the hallway. My mom, the Bozo, and I rushed out to the staircase. Our Nosy Neighbor Luisa came up from the second floor, and a guy, I don't know his name, came down from the fifth floor.

The guy from the fourth floor yelled, "I open the door and what do I see? Mr. Nicolás drawing stripes with markers next to my door, and of course, I can't tolerate that. That's going too far!"

The neighbors saw that the whole stairwell had the famous stripes. My mom was quiet, and when my mom is quiet, it's because the Earth has stopped spinning around the Sun; that's been proven.

Manolito Four-Eyes

Our Nosy Neighbor Luisa took over the case: "Mr. Nicolás, these things can be excused if a boy like Manolito does them, but when an older person does them, they throw the book at you."

I think that was my historic opportunity to say it was me, but my grandpa jumped the gun: "Ladies and gentlemen," he said, sounding like an actor in the movies, "I think I'm about to faint."

My mom grabbed his arm, and they both went into the apartment. The neighbors kept silent, not knowing what to say.

Our Nosy Neighbor Luisa, who always has to break the ice, made an emergency diagnosis: "That's from high blood pressure. My grandfather started to do foolish things because of high blood pressure. Three and a half months later, he died."

That's when I started to cry again for a whole new reason. Our Nosy Neighbor Luisa squeezed me in her arms. She wiped my tears with her hands; her hands smelled like garlic. In Our Nosy Neighbor Luisa's place, even dessert is made with garlic. I've seen it with my own glasses.

The guy from the fourth floor didn't know what to do next. No one in the building thought it was a good idea to yell at an old man with high blood pressure.

My mom came out. She freed me from Luisa's squeezing arms and wrapped her own around me. My mom's hands smelled like Limon, the dishwashing liquid we use.

My mom said, "I didn't want anyone to know, but . . . my father is senile. That's why he did that in the stairway. See, he loses his mind. We'll pay whatever it takes."

Our Nosy Neighbor Luisa said "no way"; that when all is said and done, the stripes weren't bothering anybody, and that we had to have sympathy for those poor old people who would be leaving planet Earth soon.

I was dumbfounded. Finding out that bit about your grandpa being a crazy old man who has three and a half months to live was hard for a grandson like me.

Everyone said good-bye sadly. They were almost giving us their condolences already. The guy from the fourth floor went into his apartment like the grandpa killer he'd just turned into, and we went into ours.

From that moment on, I sat in a corner watching what my grandpa did: he was dunking a stale doughnut in a glass of milk without batting an eye. He always likes stale stuff, bread or pastries, to dunk in milk with sugar. It's what he calls "the famous dunkeroo."

All of a sudden, my poor old grandpa seemed really weird. It really wasn't normal how he always preferred stale pastries, bread from the day before yesterday, and how he always looked through the fridge for leftovers from the day before. My mom says, "In my house, food doesn't get thrown away—Grandpa takes care of that. He could be on the payroll at the dump."

The truth is, I felt really bad about having a crazy

grandpa. I felt bad and scared. What if he attacked me at sundown?

Sundown came and then the night, too. Things aren't easy when you have the responsibility of sleeping with a crazy grandpa, but no one seemed to care about that.

My dad complained about dinner, as always: "Spinach again; weeds again. Catalina, you're gonna bore me to death."

And the Bozo laughed at all the foolish things my grandpa did, like every night, without knowing that they weren't foolish things, but senility due to high blood pressure.

When my mom was washing my feet for bed, I said, "Can I sleep with the Bozo?"

"What's gotten into you? You've never wanted to sleep with him before. We had to close off the terrace so you could be with your grandpa, and now you tell me you want to sleep with your brother. You're bananas."

"Is insanity hereditary?"

"You're not calling me crazy, are you?"

"No, I'm talking about grandpa."

"Oh, that one," my mom said, laughing mysteriously. "That one's cuckoo bananas."

The moment of truth had arrived. My grandpa and I in the dark room, with the radio on, like every night of our lives.

"C'mon, Manolito, sweetie. Come and heat up my feet."

He said that to me, and he gave me the ten cents for my piggy bank, like every night of our lives. And I got into the bed. Would you be brave enough to say no to a crazy old man with high blood pressure?

When my grandpa's feet were heated up, he sighed and said the same thing he always does before falling asleep: "What a relief. That changes everything."

But that night, my grandpa kept talking: "At first, I almost had cardiac arrest when the guy from the fourth floor opened his door and caught me drawing the stripes; then the dizziness thing occurred to me, and then the senility thing occurred to your mom. You can't tell me we didn't do a good job among all of us, Manolito."

My mom telling lies, my grandpa making believe he's crazy, the neighbors falling for the story, and me . . . me, too. There are times when I'm dumber than I seem at first sight.

"So, you're not crazy, and you're not gonna die in three and a half months?"

"Well, no. I'm a wreck, but I have the blood pressure of a child."

What a day! My arsenal of tears had been all used up. I hoped that the next day nothing bad would happen to me, and I wouldn't feel like committing any crimes.

One thing was clear: there were times when I didn't know why I did things.

I said, "Grandpa, I don't know why I drew on the stairwell with markers."

And my grandpa told me that we don't always know why we do things. He said that ever since markers have existed in the world, a lot of kids have drawn on walls, and none of them knew why they did it, either.

"And before markers existed?" I asked.

He said they drew on walls with pencils, and before that, with oil paints, and before that, with anything they could get their hands on.

After a lot of thinking, I said to my grandpa, "Maybe the prehistoric kid who drew animals on cave walls got chewed out, too."

"Well, maybe."

"And check it out,"—I sat up in bed because I was getting excited—"now people pay to see those."

"Go figure."

I fell asleep really happy. I think that was the happiest night of my life. Because I'd gotten out of the worst lecture of my life; because my grandpa wasn't crazy; because he wasn't going to die until 2009; and because five centuries from now specialists from all over the world would come to see the stripes at a house in Carabanchel, and there'd be pictures of my stripes in all the schoolbooks of the future.

The next day, before going to school, I took out my **Happy Holidays! Martin Fish Shop** markers and wrote really small in a corner of the stairwell:

Manolito Four-Eyes, February 2008

I wanted to make the research easier for the scientists from the twenty-fifth century, and I wanted my name to be seen in all the books.

When all is said and done, my grandpa helped, but I was the inventor and the artist.

9

World Peace

Seven days and seven nights ago, Miss Asunción came into class at nine o'clock on the dot—not giving us those five minutes we usually have every morning to throw in each other's faces what we did the day before.

Miss Asunción took a breath, and almost all of us yawned because it was pretty early to deal with one of her speeches.

She said the following: "We're going to try out for a costume contest that's going to be held in a club here in town next Saturday. Children from schools the whole town over are going to audition, and you have to show the whole world that you're proper children and not the delinquents you seem—"

We didn't let her finish. There was a mad rush in the class like you wouldn't believe.

Ozzy the Bully got up to say, "A warning: I'm gonna dress up as Superman, and I'm telling you now so that no one else dresses up as Superman. In this galaxy, there's only one Superman and that's me, and I don't want to have to split anyone's face open. I repeat: this is a warning."

So Big Ears said, "And what am I supposed to dress up as if I only have a Superman costume, and my mom's not gonna wanna buy me another one?"

And then you heard the entire class echo: "Me, too . . . me, too . . . me, too . . ." because all the kids have had the same Superman costume for centuries and centuries.

But Ozzy had given a warning. He lunged for the first kid he could grab. In those moments of high atmospheric pressure, Ozzy is uncontrollable—he doesn't care if there are eight kids or eighty. I don't know why he had to grab me; maybe my mom's right when she says I'm always in the middle, like Wednesday.

Luckily, I'm a kid with reflexes, and I quickly defended myself: "You don't have to break my glasses this time, Ozzy. Everyone knows I'd rather be Spider-Man."

Then a kid from my class said he was Spider-Man, and a girl who wanted to be Beauty yelled that she needed a Beast. . . . The way things were going, we didn't have any other choice but to fight each other—it's the only way we have in my class to solve our problems of coexistence.

Miss Asunción flipped her lid right outta Madrid,

banging on the desk three times, which made us remember all at once that we were in school, in class, with a ruthless teacher. She said there'd be no Supermen or Spider-Men, or Beauties or Beasts; that we had to prove to Carabanchel, to Spain, to the United States, and to planet Earth that we were good kids and that we fought for peace in the world-wide world; and that she'd planned on all thirty of us dressing up as white doves.

Because Miss Asunción was armed with her pointer, and was our teacher, too, and because we're a bunch of cowards, we didn't say in unison: "Get outta town, clown."

But we were really disappointed—it was the biggest

bummer of our existence. We got really quiet, now that we had nothing to look forward to in the worldwide world.

Then Our Teach went on: "The jury from the Neighbors' Association will give us first prize. There isn't a jury in Spain that could resist giving first prize to thirty kids dressed up as white doves. We'll get a lot of gifts, too. For one day, we'll be symbols of World Peace—but until Saturday, our war cry will be: 'We're gonna pulverize 'em!'"

Now *that* we did like. With a war cry like that, we could go to the ends of the Earth. We were going to *pulverize* all the kids from all the schools in town with our super white-dove outfits.

That week, my mom and the mothers of the twenty-nine other kids made us dove outfits out of tissue paper. My mom complained a lot; she says that for Miss Asunción, any excuse is good enough to have her spending money and working extra. She said she'd bought me the Spider-Man costume so she wouldn't have to worry about another costume until the day I started my military service and they gave me a soldier uniform. And she said it was peace that *she* needed, a lot of peace on a deserted beach without kids—in her opinion, that's what World Peace was all about.

She stayed quiet for thirty milliseconds, and then she kept complaining and saying that if I couldn't keep still, I could never try on my dove costume. You have to be very careful with me because costumes never fit over my head.

"This kid," she said, referring to me, "he might not have much, but he was born with a foot-long forehead."

My grandpa consoled her, and me, by saying, "Just like Einstein. All geniuses have always had foot-long foreheads."

She had to make another dove outfit for the Bozo since the Bozo is "monkey see, monkey do," and if he doesn't get the same costume as I do, he's gotten into the habit of not eating. My mom says one day he's going to dehydrate on us. I don't care if he does dehydrate, but she doesn't want to hear that.

At last, *C* day arrived—*C* for Contest and for Carabanchel. My mom dressed us in our tissue-paper suits and told us to get going to school. She really liked seeing us leave the house dressed up as World Peace and holding hands. Don't ask me why; I could never explain it.

We ran into Our Nosy Neighbor Luisa on the stairway, and she said to us, "Look at all the trouble your mother went through to dress you up as penguins."

I had no other choice but to grab the Bozo and go back up to my house to tell my mom that we weren't going outside as penguins—even if it was for World Peace. My mom said that if Our Nosy Neighbor Luisa couldn't distinguish between a penguin and a dove, that was her problem, to get moving to school, and why did we constantly have to show up late everywhere?

Out on the street, the first thing I heard was one

woman say to another, "Look at those gorgeous penguins!"

But I didn't want to go back home. My mom, in certain moments of her life, can get bad tempered, and when all is said and done, we were representing World Peace, after all.

When we got to school, we were stunned: Ozzy was at the door dressed up with some feathers like a chicken; Big Ears looked like a turkey; the One-and-Only Susana looked like an ostrich; Paquito Medina, a pelican; and so on up to twenty-nine. There were no two birds alike. Well, except the Bozo and me: a pair of gorgeous penguins.

My grandpa, who'd just shown up, said, "Alfred Hitchcock should've seen this to make *The Birds: Part Two*."

We all stood there looking at each other, really peeved.

Miss Asunción wasn't left out. She arrived dressed up, too, and she looked like a duck—or a goose. Flapping her wings, she told us the festival was going to be broadcast on Radio Carabanchel, which is a radio program they do in my neighborhood—since there's no money for microphones, my grandpa says they do the programs by the old system of opening the window and shouting.

Miss Asunción didn't seem to mind that we didn't match, or maybe she didn't notice. As she escorted us to Club Silicone, where the festival was being held, she was so happy that she didn't seem like Our Teach. If we hadn't been dressed as big ol' birds, we would have cracked up laughing. She told us that when she came out on stage, she'd say, "One, two, three . . . !"

And we would answer by flapping our wings and shouting all at once until our throats broke, "Long live World Peace!"

Our Teach wanted us to practice, so right there in the street, she screeched like a nut, "One, two, three . . . !"

We were going to scream, "Long live World Peace!" but when we flapped our wings, we got all tangled up, and if Our Teach hadn't straightened us out, we would have

shown up at the club totally plucked. She told us to forget about flapping our wings; we'd flap them after winning the prize.

When we got to the club, the thirty of us and the Bozo sat down in a corner. The presenter was the principal of Primpers Preschool, which is next to my house. The guy was dressed up as Superman. Ozzy the Bully ground his teeth from the filthy envy he felt. I took advantage of the occasion to brown-nose my friend Ozzy a little.

I said, "That guy can't be Superman with the gut he

has. A guy with a gut like that couldn't fly over Niagara Falls because the force of gravity on our planet attracts bodies like that one."

"What would happen?" asked Ozzy, who was mega-interested in my theories.

"He'd splatter against the ground."

Ozzy was not only very impressed with my deep scientific knowledge, but also very happy. The "he'd splatter against the ground" bit had given Ozzy back his usual optimism. He wasn't jealous anymore; now he looked down his feathers at the Superman presenter—like how a professional superhero looks at a movie superhero.

Supergut began announcing the school groups that came onstage, amid the boos from all of us who were sitting. As you'd understand, we weren't about to applaud our enemies. Remember, our motto was "We're gonna pulverize 'em!"

Some kids came out dressed as trees. The group was called "Autumn." They each had a chain that was hanging from a branch. They pulled on the chains, and their leaves fell automatically. The audience was silenced by the baloney they'd just seen. That group's parents were the only ones who applauded, of course. The rest of us just watched as they spent ten minutes on stage picking up their fallen leaves.

Then the classic superheroes came out, and kids dressed up as reality shows, and others dressed up as chocolate croissants . . .

We were the fifth ones out. We were trained for Miss Asunción's "One, two, three . . . !" and our "Long live World Peace!" But we didn't have time to do our number because when she shouted "One, two, three . . . !"—we heard another voice after hers. It was the voice of a kid from Baronesa Thyssen, the professional drama school in my neighborhood, and what he shouted was:

"Ozzy, that chicken outfit fits you great!"

In an instant, Ozzy the Bully flung himself off the stage to turn that jokester's face inside out. The One-and-Only Susana was right behind her boyfriend, and all the rest of us were behind the One-and-Only Susana— because if we don't defend Ozzy, later on it'll be us who need defending.

The jokester's father said, "My boy is partly right: Ozzy looks like a chicken when he's supposed to be a dove, and no matter how badly the costume fits, that is intolerable."

Poor Miss Asunción was alone up on the stage, crying in her duck costume. We had to separate our parents from the Baronesa Thyssen parents because they were about to get rude, and when all was said and done, someone had to represent World Peace.

This day had the potential of being the worst day of our lives, but you're not going to believe what ended up happening—because what ended up happening could not have been expected, even by the Martians on Earth.

Once the fight died down and the stage cleared, Supergut came out and tried to make like he was flying (I guess to entertain us; it wasn't clear). The guy just about killed himself in one of his attempts to take off. Obviously, if it were so easy, everyone would be a superhero—gimme a break. But we should've thanked him for his stumble: it was what the audience liked most the whole afternoon.

Ozzy explained to some kids from another school: "That guy can't be Superman. Earth's 'course of poverty' would make him splatter against the ground."

"The course of poverty!" Ozzy is such an animal—the only word he managed to learn correctly from my theory was the famous "splatter." But don't go thinking I called his attention to it. If I corrected him, then I, too, would've known what it was like to splatter against this planet.

Supergut called out the prizes, going from the third to the first to make the moment even more exciting:

"The third prize goes to the group 'Reality Shows,' for its congeniality and originality."

The entire audience broke out in boos: "Get out!!!"

"We've awarded the second prize to the group 'Autumn,' for the beauty in its representation of a season."

Did he say "for the beauty"? I told Ozzy that this jury deserved to be thrown over Niagara Falls, followed by Supergut, of course. Once again, we agreed. All of a sudden, the biggest bully in my class and I agreed on everything— I was his best friend. I was pretty proud of myself. When the biggest bully in school is your best friend, it means your back is covered; it's as if you have Aladdin's genie at your command, ready to defend you against any enemy.

"And the first prize . . ." Supergut paused to create more anticipation; I guarantee you that you could hear the anxious spectators grind their teeth. "We've awarded the first prize by unanimous decision to the group 'The Birds,' for their defense of the different species in danger of extinction."

Since nobody went up, the presenter had to repeat it. We all just looked at each other—hadn't we come for World Peace?

But no one else had figured out the World Peace part, so we had to admit that we were a group of birds in danger of extinction.

You can't always be what you want in this life.

They made us go out onstage again to accept the prize. The prize was in a big box. The Bozo tried to open it by biting it. With all the racket, we were plucking our feathers again, but we didn't care about that anymore. We didn't have the responsibility of representing World Peace: we were only birds.

Our Teach cleared the way by pinching us treacherously, and she opened the box with her powerful hands. Supergut called for a big applause. The prize was . . . school supplies—books, notebooks, and stuff like that. All the bore galore about World Peace to win more books to study! The only one who applauded was the Bozo. You have to forgive him for his ignorance; since he hasn't studied in the time he's been on this planet, he didn't know what they were.

We left the stage. There was nothing else for us to do there. Miss Asunción could keep the gift and eat it with french fries. She was thrilled by all the books and no doubt planning new homework to destroy our brains.

Our parents were proud of their children in danger of extinction. In the afternoon, mine said I could go down to Hangman's Park. I dressed up in my Spider-Man costume.

My mom said to Our Nosy Neighbor Luisa, "Kids are like that. They're easy—A, B, C and one, two, three and don't take that away from them. They put on their super-hero costumes, and they're all happy."

I thought of climbing down the wall of my building—but I'm a boy who's conscious of his limitations, and I knew that the only thing I had in common with Spider-Man was the costume. When I arrived at Hangman's Park, my friends were already waiting for me: Ozzy dressed as Superman; Big Ears as Superman, but without the cape because it was his job to be Superman's assistant; the

One-and-Only Susana as Beauty, even though as soon as you're around her, you realize she's the Beast in disguise; and Paquito Medina as Robin Hood. The Bozo showed up soon after me, still wearing his penguin outfit because my mom had convinced him it was the nicest one in the neighborhood (at that age you still believe the lies that mothers tell).

We played superheroes, of course. We made two teams. Ozzy picked me to be on his team. I asked him if he thought our war cry should be: "We're gonna pulverize 'em for World Peace." He thought it was the bee's knees. It was obvious that I'd become his great friend. We played kick the can, bubonic plague, and leapfrog, which is a game that consists of one team crouching down and the other one throwing themselves on top mercilessly; it's one of those games they call "educational." I did everything I could; I ran and I held up with all my strength, but the others always managed to beat me. It's the only defect I find in games with running and strength—I always get beaten. When Ozzy realized that with me on his team he was goin' nowhere fast, he decided that nobody would be on teams. Ozzy was only interested in beating Paquito Medina, anyway. Beating Big Ears, the One-and-Only Susana, the Bozo, or me isn't exciting for Ozzy.

I grabbed the Bozo by the hand, and we went home. I really left because I couldn't hold back the desire to cry. I'd gone from being Ozzy's great friend to being a sewer rat, and that's something that would bug anyone. The

Bozo saw me cry and he started crying, too. With him, everything's contagious—the good and the bad—that's what my mom says. We had to share a handkerchief. I blew my nose first, and then I put the handkerchief up to his nose. He did what he always does: prepares himself by concentrating hard, breathes in, and then sniffs in the boogies instead of blowing them out. It's his style. And I had to laugh, even though I had tears in my eyes—you have to admit, even though he's the Bozo, he's pretty funny, too. He had to take after me in some way.

In the middle of it all, Paquito Medina came running up to us.

"What are you doing?" he asked.

"Crying from laughing so hard," I answered. Did you really think I was going to confess the truth to him?

Paquito Medina asked me if I wanted to go over to his house on Sunday to play on his computer.

And I asked him, "Are you gonna invite Ozzy, too?"

"Ozzy might break it. He's an animal."

So I said I would. The truth is that it would be a bore galore playing with Paquito Medina on the computer—because Paquito Medina wins at everything, just like I lose at everything—but I didn't care. The smartest guy I'd ever met in my life wanted to invite *only me*. Why? Because Manolito Four-Eyes doesn't break computers; because Manolito Four-Eyes isn't an animal like some people; because Manolito Four-Eyes is a guy you can trust 100 percent. It was obvious that Paquito Medina had decided I was his great friend. It was one of the happiest moments of my life.

I felt like maybe I really could climb up the wall of my building in my Spider-Man costume, but I didn't—my mom doesn't like the Bozo to go up the stairs alone. The Bozo and I raced to our apartment. I beat him. There are two people in the worldwide world that I can outrun: the Bozo and my Grandpa Nicolás. So what? There are worse things.

When we were putting our pajamas on later, my grandpa said to us: "One, two, three . . ."

And the Bozo and I shouted with all our might, "Long live World Peace!"

We were having a terrific time until the royal-pain upstairs neighbor came down to complain about the racket.

Our Teach's famous motto always brought problems to our lives.

10

A Happy Birthday

My grandpa didn't want to celebrate his birthday. He said no, no, and no.

My mom said, "But, Dad, you don't turn eighty every day."

"Thank God," said my grandpa. "All I'd need is that aggravation."

"C'mon, Grandpa," I said. "We'll set it up; you invite your friends; we'll buy a piñata. . . ." I was already picturing it.

"And inside the piñata you can put arthritis pills, incontinence pills, high blood pressure pills . . ."—my grandpa felt like seeing the bad side of everything—

". . . not to mention, prostate pills. If I invite my friends, this place will be full of old geezers, dentures, bunions. . . . I don't want to. And anyway, what friends do I have?"

"Ozzy's grandfather," I said.

"If I told Ozzy's grandfather to come to my birthday party, he'd pee his pants laughing. Old people don't celebrate birthdays. That's never been done before. Do you want me to blow out eighty candles, too?"

"Yeah!" said the Bozo and I, because sometimes we agree.

"I blow out eighty candles, and you'll have to bury me after 'Happy Birthday.'"

That got the Bozo and me to start singing "Happy Birthday." We always sing that kind of song in duet, kicking the table legs. It's our style: the melodic song.

My grandpa stuck to his guns: "And the kicker is, when you're old, people only give you scarves. They fill your closet with scarves. Not one tie, not one bottle of cologne, not one three-quarter jacket—just scarves."

"Well, tell us what you *want* us to give you." My mom doesn't give up so easily, either.

"Nothing! I don't have anything to celebrate. I don't have friends, and I don't feel like turning eighty. The only things I have are scarves from my last birthdays."

Having said that, my grandpa went to the bathroom to put in his dentures. He was going out to get some sun with Ozzy's grandfather. My grandpa's not the type to get some sun without teeth. He slammed the door and left. The Bozo and I were left in mid-"Happy Birthday."

I'd never known anybody who didn't want to celebrate his birthday. Even my mom, who's wanted to turn thirty-seven for the past five years, wants to celebrate it; and she lets you know several days before—so that my dad remembers and buys her a diamond, a mink, or a blender with some killer blades: which is the only thing he ever ends up buying her.

After my grandpa slammed the door, I thought my mom was going to get mad. If there's one thing in life she doesn't like, it's when you go against her. The Bozo and I stayed really quiet. In those moments, it's easy to mess up over the littlest thing; if you sneeze a little too hard, heads will roll, and not exactly from the sneeze. But no, my mom didn't get mad; she kept clearing the table as if nothing had happened. As my dad says, "She's unpredictable."

The unpredictable mom didn't mention my grandpa's birthday again, and the famous *G* day—*G* for grandpa—was getting dangerously close. The eve of that mysterious Wednesday, my mom called me to her room and closed the door. I immediately began trembling, and I said:

"I didn't do it on purpose. It was the Bozo who took the snack cakes from the minibar. He wanted to see how they would splatter if we threw them off the balcony." It turned out that the one I threw hit Our Nosy Neighbor

Luisa on her hunchback hump.

"I didn't call you about that, Manolito."

There are times in life when I jump the gun with an apology, and that was one of them. For the first time in history, she didn't call me to chew me out. She said that she was going to celebrate my grandpa's birthday—over his dead body or anyone else's.

"But he doesn't want to—"

"What he wants or doesn't want doesn't matter."

That's how my mom is—not even the Pope is capable of making her change plans. I'd like to see the Pope try to tell my mom to celebrate a birthday or not. My mom is the maximum authority on the planet; even extraterrestrials like Paquito Medina know that.

My mom cooked up a plan, a perfect plan, the most perfect plan a mom has cooked up since life has existed on the global Earth. The plan consisted of the following:

a) I'd go with my grandpa to take the Bozo to the doctor. Why were we taking the Bozo to the doctor, you ask? Because he had a stuffy nose. But it didn't matter; if it hadn't been the stuffed-up nose, it would've been something else. The Bozo is a kid who's always at the doctor. He catches everything. Why? Because he sucks up all the crap on the ground. But let's ditch that story. If I told you all the nasty things the Bozo does, you wouldn't be able to eat again in your whole life.

b) While we're at the doctor, my mom would go to the supermarket to buy provisions for the magnificent, colossal Feast.

c) Six in the afternoon, in the apartment—the guests would be: my dad, my mom, Our Nosy Neighbor Luisa, Our Nosy Neighbor Luisa's husband, me, and the Bozo.

What a bore galore of a birthday! I asked my mom if she'd told Ozzy's grandpa about it, but my mom remembered that my grandpa had said he was embarrassed to invite an old friend. Well, she said, forget it—no old friend.

Before I left the room, she added, "And let me find out you're throwing snack cakes off the terrace again, and you'll go over with them."

I knew it was impossible to go into my mom's room and not mess it up somehow. But I came out safe and sound, so I couldn't complain.

Having such a fat secret in my brain made me really nervous. There were moments that day when it seemed like the secret didn't fit in my head.

When we were going to bed, I said to my grandpa, "Tomorrow is your birthday, but we'll never celebrate it."

My grandpa said "Good," and he closed his eyes to sleep. There are times when he's a terrible, cold-blooded man.

The next day I opened my pig's guts. Generally, people

break the ceramic piggy bank when it's full; but since I never expect to fill it and I always want to open it when two or three coins jingle inside, my dad made a secret slot in the belly and everyone's happy: I don't have to break the piggy bank, and they don't have to buy me a new one every Sunday.

I had thirty cents. It wasn't much. The truth is that I had only been saving for a weekend; that's not even enough to buy those scarves my grandpa said were so repulsive. If I had enough money, I would've liked to buy him new dentures. The ones he had were made a hair too big, and if he ate something hard, it was a worldwide disaster: he'd end up taking out his teeth with the piece of meat stuck in the dentures.

I took the thirty cents to school. I was about to spend them at the Blue Booth—Mr. Mariano's booth, which has all the cheap candies and toys known throughout the world. I wanted a bag of red marbles from China, but I backed out—ever since the Bozo almost choked on my marbles, my mom considers them pretty prohibited. Forget about the marbles. Then I saw some bags that had Viking warriors, but you see, Mr. Mariano's Viking warriors don't stand up, and I like the ones that stand up, in order to make the pillow into a mountain of Vikings, like in the movies. Forget about the Vikings. Then I saw a top, but I already had one. A yo-yo—already had it. . . . Bet you don't know what I saw all of a sudden, without prior warning? *Dracula teeth!* I didn't have money for teeth from the dentist, but I did have money to buy my grandpa fangs. At that moment, I was the best person I'd known in

my entire life, no exaggeration. I was like a boy in a story who's capable of dying to save his grandpa. (Thank God, I wasn't really obligated to die—because, the truth is, I would've thought twice about it.)

At recess, Ozzy asked me if I would lend him my teeth. I gave them to him for a while, but I asked him not to suck on them too much because I was going to give them to my grandpa. Then Paquito Medina put them on, and so did Big Ears, who left them full of chocolate croissant. I cleaned them on his pants, and they ended up just as white as before: they were top-quality teeth.

When we were in class, I remembered that my grandpa had said he didn't want a birthday with old geezers, so I thought it would be a great idea to invite my friends instead. My friends might have a lot of defects (they *all* do), but they're not old geezers. I secretly passed around a note to them. Our Teach doesn't like you to start inviting people to a birthday while she's explaining a bore galore about the climates of the world. We had to wait till after class to discuss it. I thought maybe my friends wouldn't be up for going to a grandfather's birthday . . . but yes, they all said Yes! My friends are capable of going to King Kong's birthday, as long as there's cake and Coke. I told them they'd all have to come over after school to take the Bozo to the doctor first. "Well, all right then, we'll go to the doctor first," they said.

At home at lunchtime, the Bozo and I sang "Happy

Birthday" again to my grandpa, and we watched TV as if nothing else in the world mattered to us. (There are times when what matters most to us *is* the TV, but on this occasion, we were faking.)

When I returned to school after lunch, Ozzy was with his grandpa on the steps.

Ozzy said, "My grandpa wants to know why your grandpa didn't invite him to his birthday party."

"It's just that my grandpa thinks that birthday parties aren't for old geezers."

"Well, it's gonna backfire on him," said Ozzy's grandpa. "I'm sick and tired of treating him in Stumbles just so he can leave me out in the cold on the street. What time is the lousy party?"

"Six o'clock," I said.

It was obvious that my grandpa's opinion was not sacred—everyone blew it off.

These were the final ingredients of my mom's perfect plan:

a) My grandpa, me, Big Ears, Paquito Medina, Ozzy the Bully, and the One-and-Only Susana would go to the clinic so the doctor could examine the Bozo's stuffy nose—a spectacle comparable only to *The Matrix*.

b) Ozzy's grandpa would be at my house with his teeth in at six o'clock. There, he'd meet up with my parents, Our Nosy Neighbor Luisa, and her husband. My mom would ask herself, "And who invited this one?" But she'd keep quiet because in front of guests, she's always very polite, like Lady Di.

c) The magnificent, colossal Feast would be awaiting us on the table.

When my grandpa came to pick me up from school with the Bozo and discovered all of us were going to the doctor with him, he was dumbstruck—but he kept quiet. He's used to us doing worse things, like the day Big Ears and I switched a black olive for a cockroach in Stumbles. We speared it with a toothpick and everything; it could've passed for an olive, but my grandpa suspected that he wasn't dealing with an everyday olive when he saw its legs moving. (Cockroaches are as common in Stumbles as olives, anyway.)

We had a terrific time in the waiting room of the clinic. It's fantastic to go to the doctor when it's someone else's turn to be examined. We skated down the halls; we spun around like tops; we played leapfrog; and when we wanted to laugh like animals, we asked the Bozo, "How are you gonna show the doctor you blow your nose?" And the Bozo would enter into a state of concentration and then sniff in the boogies instead of blowing out.

My friends split their sides watching the Bozo perform his load of baloney, and the Bozo got excited being the center of attention; and from sniffing in the boogies so much, he turned bright red, and he almost wound up staying that way, like my mom always warns us. Then we all went together into the office of Doctor Morales, who is the doctor of all my friends and cures almost all illnesses and who, according to the mothers, is a hottie and a riot. Doctor Morales is like a doctor on TV—all of Carabanchel agrees on that. Our whole crew got on the stretcher with the Bozo; everything seemed to go really well until Ozzy wanted to tip over the stretcher and throw us off. Then the nice Doctor Morales, the TV doctor, asked us if we didn't have anything better to do at home.

Big Ears, who got stuck with the role in life of putting his foot in his mouth, said, "Yeah, we have to celebrate the birthday of—"

He couldn't finish his deadly sentence because he discovered that four elbows were stuck in his mouth.

The doctor's diagnosis calmed us down a lot—the Bozo's boogies weren't serious; they were disgusting. All of a sudden, I realized that it was already six fifteen! We all grabbed my grandpa, tugging on his suit jacket, and we practically ran him back to my house. Once in a while, we got the nervous giggles—because the excitement of bringing a grandpa to a surprise birthday party can only be compared to Niagara Falls or the Grand Canyon—nothing else in life is as exciting.

When we buzzed the intercom at my apartment, my mom's voice came on, saying, "Manolito, tell your grandpa to go over to Stumbles to get a bottle of soda water for dinner."

My grandpa turned around to go to Stumbles. He loves when my mom sends him to the bar for something she forgot. What happens next is that he forgets to peel himself away from the bar to come back home.

I went up to my apartment with my friends. My mom opened the door and stood there looking at us: "All of these?"

With my friends, she doesn't hold back one smidgen; she treats them just as badly as if they were her own children.

"Since grandpa didn't want a birthday full of old geezers, I brought him my friends," I explained.

"It doesn't matter," my mom said in a suspicious tone. "We have kids, old people . . . It's a birthday for all audiences."

It was true. It had occurred to Ozzy's grandpa to bring four other grandpas who go to play bridge at the senior center. Our Nosy Neighbor Luisa was there, too, but that's nothing new; Our Nosy Neighbor Luisa is always at our place, except at bedtime, when she goes down to her husband in case his toupee falls out of place when he snores.

My mother seated us around the table. You couldn't even touch a Cheeto because they'd all been counted; my mom gets nervous when there are a lot of people and a little food. Everyone was all set to sing "Happy Birthday" as soon as Grandpa peeked in from the door.

We heard his key, and we started to sing like nuts and eat at the same time. Before the footsteps got to the living room, Ozzy had already finished the chips and his glass of Coke; and he managed that in my apartment which, as my mom says, is a matchbox. But the one who came in wasn't my grandpa—it was Our Nosy Neighbor Luisa's husband, who came with more provisions: three bottles of wine for the old folks. My mom said that the next person to lunge at the food would get a sandwich so he could go eat it in Hangman's Park, alone and sad. She's a mom without compassion.

Our Nosy Neighbor Luisa's husband staked out his position in our chorus around the table. We heard the key in the door again, and we repeated our "Happy Birthday" with the same powerful energy. Ozzy kept stuffing food in his mouth, thinking my mom didn't know. Of course, he was wrong. She always knows—it's just that sometimes she decides to wait. If I were God, I'd put her on the payroll:

she's capable of having her eyes everywhere. She's one of those chameleon types.

Another whopping disappointment: it was my dad, who came with a block of Spain's famous Manchego cheese that he'd bought in a restaurant on the highway. My mom cut some golden wedges of cheese and passed them around so we could nibble on something while the protagonist of our true story had yet to arrive.

We got ourselves back in our positions, and we ate the cheese without making any noise, so that when my grandpa came in he wouldn't figure out that his home had been invaded by thousands of people. A while went by, another while . . . and by the third while, the old folks asked for chairs because the truth is, my grandpa was starting to be a bit of a pain in the neck.

My mom decided to call Stumbles. She has the bar's phone number memorized since she has to rescue my grandpa a lot.

The owner, Mr. Ezequiel, picked up and told my mom, "Well, yes, Mr. Nicolás is here. He just treated me to some red wine for his birthday. He says that nobody has even given him so much as one miserable scarf."

My mom answered, "Tell my father to come up immediately."

And my grandpa came up immediately. When my mom says "immediately," there's no such Earthling who would dare come up "in a while."

The living-room door opened, and we began our "Happy Birthday" for the millionth time. We did it better than the kids who sing for the Pope; if the Pope knew us, he'd put *us* on the payroll. You should've seen the look on my grandpa's face when he saw that all of Spain was in the living room of our apartment. Mr. Ezequiel came in after him, with one tray of shrimp and another of clams, and everyone welcomed *him* with a big round of applause. I don't think the trays lasted even fifty milliseconds. The old folks ate the shrimp with the shell on and the clams by the handful. People took out gifts: Ozzy's grandpa's gift was a checkered scarf that my grandpa loved; the other old folks gave him two scarves, a black one and a green one that my grandpa said were beautiful; Our Nosy Neighbor Luisa bought him a scarf "made in Italy" that we all thought was really elegant; my mom gave him a foulard, which is like a scarf but made of cloth "so you look younger," and everyone agreed that he looked ten years younger; my friends promised him scarves for his next birthday; and the Bozo and I gave him the Dracula teeth, which were a megasuccess. My grandpa said that they would be his Sunday teeth. My grandpa was a cool vampire—the famous Vampire of Carabanchel, that's my grandpa.

There was nothing left: no more wine, soda, water, shrimp, clams. They went down for more, but it kept disappearing. The old folks were in line to pee the whole time; when it was the last one in the line's turn, the first one had to go again.

My mom took the cake out, but you couldn't see the cake: it was hidden by eighty candles. My mom lowered the shades so that the living room would be lit up only by the glow of all the candles. The Bozo cried because he was scared of the old folks' candlelit faces. The fangs stuck out of both sides of my grandpa's mouth. It was really spooky; the only thing missing was a drop of blood on his chin. My mom told the kids to blow out the candles. We yelled "One, two, three!"—but then Ozzy jumped the gun and blew out almost all of them himself. Even at your grandpa's party, there's a guy who messes up your life. My mom said that you shouldn't fight at birthday parties, so I had to put up with it, as usual. (Now that I think of it, I could care less about blowing out candles—how dopey.) While they cut the cake, we sang "For he's a jolly good fellow." My grandpa shed two or three tears, as he always does whenever there's a toast (or when the clock in the Puerta del Sol strikes for New Year's and everyone eats twelve grapes for good luck—he loves that). Ozzy's grandpa said that my grandpa had to say a few words. My grandpa said no, no, and no, but there was a chorus of "Speech! Speech!" So my grandpa broke some news, the best news of the season considering that Real Madrid wouldn't win the League Championships if they kept playing the way they'd been playing.

My grandpa announced, "I've always said that I plan on dying in 2009. But I think, instead, I'm gonna try two or three years of the next decade."

And the audience applauded. My mom asked all of us to go down to Hangman's Park while she cleaned up. The floor was full of chips and Coke. Yet without a doubt, by nighttime it would be as shiny as a mirror again—because my mom is like those moms on commercials, but with a much smaller apartment.

So we went down to Hangman's Park. After a while, the mothers came to pick up my friends. The Bozo, my

grandpa, and I were the last ones there. I didn't have to wear the dreaded peacoat anymore, and the days had grown much longer. That meteorological change happens every year in Carabanchel on the fourteenth of April, my grandpa's birthday. Don't ask me why. Scientists from all over the world have tried to find an explanation for this phenomenon, and they haven't found it, but they have to admit that summer in Carabanchel starts the day Grandpa Nicolás turns a year older.

My grandpa had taken all of his scarves in a bag, to look at them every now and again. I do the same thing with the gifts from my birthday parties: I take all of them down to Hangman's Park so they're not away from me the whole day. We were sitting on the only bench in Hangman's Park that's not broken; it's the bench where all the grandpas take a nap every morning. The one who fell asleep was the Bozo; he had his head resting on my grandpa and his feet on me. I always have to put up with the worst in people. The Bozo is really small, but his feet already smell; he takes after my dad that way.

But I take after my dad, too: with my glasses and with my name.

I was really happy, thinking about how there weren't many days to go before school ended, and the ruthless Miss Asunción would disappear for a few months. When summer came, my grandpa, the Bozo, and I would go down to the park with my friends every day until it got dark—without a jacket, without a coat, without anything. Our moms would call us from the terraces when the sausages were ready, and everyone in my neighborhood would go to bed much later.

It was two hundred pounds of cool that summer was coming.

My grandpa pointed to the bright red sun about to disappear behind Hangman's Tree. My grandpa says that the ground in Carabanchel is horrible, but the sky is one of the most beautiful in the world, as beautiful as the pyramids of Egypt or the Empire State Building. It's the eighth wonder of the worldwide world.

Everything was as quiet as in a movie where a grandpa and a boy are the last ones in the cemetery after a funeral. But this was much better—because in the movie of my life, my grandpa had promised me that he would try the next decade.

You're not gonna believe it, but I think it was the happiest day of my existence on planet Earth.

THE END

Look for more adventures of
Manolito Four-Eyes and his family
and friends coming to bookstores
in Spring 2009.

ELVIRA LINDO's series about the adventures of Manolito Four-Eyes is a children's classic in Spain, where it has inspired feature films and a TV series, as well as in other European countries. She has received Spain's National Children's Book Award, and her books are regularly translated into some twenty languages. She also works as a screenwriter, and her weekly column in *El País* newspaper is widely read in Spain and Latin America. She lives half of the year in New York City.

EMILIO URBERUAGA is a writer and illustrator in Spain whose work has been published all over the world.

JOANNE MORIARTY grew up in Quincy, Massachusetts, and currently resides in Brooklyn. She is a Spanish interpreter at New York Presbyterian Hospital in Manhattan.